THE APSLEY HOUSE INCIDENT

TRACY GRANT

The Apsley House Incident

Ebook ISBN: 9781641971836
KDP POD ISBN:
IS POD ISBN: 9781641971898

NYLA Publishing
121 W 27th St., Suite 1201, New York, NY 10001
http://www.nyliterary.com

For Deirdre, Chris, Sierra, and Piper

ACKNOWLEDGMENTS

The Apsley House Incident is my third work written entirely during the COVID-19 pandemic. I am more grateful than ever for the wonderful people who support me and my daughter and the Rannochs and their world in so many ways. As always, huge thanks to my wonderful agent, Nancy Yost, for her support and insights, and eagle-eye with copy. Thank you to Natanya Wheeler for once again working her magic to create a cover that brings my rough notes to life and beautifully evokes Mélanie Rannoch and for shepherding the book expertly through the publication process, to Sarah Younger for superlative social media support and for helping the book along through production and publication, and to the entire team at Nancy Yost Literary Agency for their fabulous work. Malcolm, Mélanie, and I are all very fortunate to have their support.

Thanks to Eve Lynch for the meticulous and thoughtful copyediting and to Kristen Loken for a magical author photo taken in one of my favorite places, San Francisco's War Memorial Opera House, on one of my favorite occasions of the year, the Merola Grand Finale. Just a few weeks ago, my daughter Mélanie and I went back there for a performance for the first time in almost two years.

I am very fortunate to have a wonderful group of writer friends near and far who make being a writer less solitary, even— or especially—during the pandemic. Thanks to Lauren Willig for guest hosting a wonderful virtual book party and conversation about the series—and for sharing the joys of historical research and the challenges of juggling life as a writer and a mom. To Penelope Williamson, for sharing adventures, analyzing plots, and being a wonderful honorary aunt to my daughter. So glad we were recently able to travel together again. To Jami Alden, Tasha Alexander, Bella Andre, Allison Brennan, Josie Brown, Isobel Carr, Catherine Coulter, Deborah Coonts, Deborah Crombie, Carol Culver/Grace, Catherine Duthie, Alexandra Elliott, J.T. Ellison, Barbara Freethy, Andrew Grant, C.S. Harris, Candice Hern, Anne Mallory, Monica McCarty, Brenda Novak, Poppy Reifiin, Deanna Raybourn, and Veronica Wolff. Thank you to the #momswritersclub on Twitter for bimonthly chats that are energizing and inspiring, and especially to Jessica Payne for starting it and to Jessica and Sara Read for their wonderful #MomsWritersClub YouTube channel on which Mélanie and I had the fun of doing a guest interview.

Thank you to the readers who support Malcolm and Mélanie and their friends and provide wonderful insights on my Web site and social media, and especially on the Goodreads Discussion Group for the series..

Thanks to Gregory Paris and jim saliba for creating and updating a fabulous Web site that chronicles Malcolm and Mélanie's adventures. Thanks to my colleagues at the Merola Opera Program who help me keep my life in balance—even on Zoom, I love spending time with you. And thanks to Mélanie herself, for inspiring my writing, being patient with Mummy's "work time", and offering her own insights at the keyboard. One of my proudest moments was when she said "Can I borrow your computer? I want to type the story I'm writing." I am so proud that my website now includes "Mélanie's Corner" for her stories, starting with her wonderful series *Talea's Mysteries*. This is Mélanie's contribution to this story – "this is the best day ever and my mom is abugilleean times better!!!"

DRAMATIS PERSONAE

*indicates real historical figures

The Rannoch Family & Household

Mélanie Suzanne Rannoch, playwright and former French intelligence agent
Malcolm Rannoch, her husband, MP and former British intelligence agent
Colin Rannoch, their son
Jessica Rannoch, their daughter
Berowne, their cat

Laura O'Roarke, Colin and Jessica's former governess, teacher, and writer
Raoul O'Roarke, her husband, Mélanie's former spymaster, and Malcolm's father
Lady Emily Fitzwalter, Laura's daughter from her first marriage
Clara O'Roarke, Laura and Raoul's daughter

Gisèle Thirle, Malcolm's sister

Andrew Thirle, her husband
Ian Thirle, their son

Alistair Rannoch (Alexander Radford), Malcolm and Gisèle's supposed father, Elsinore League founder

The Davenport Family
Lady Cordelia Davenport, classicist
Colonel Harry Davenport, her husband, classicist, former British intelligence agent
Livia Davenport, their daughter
Drusilla Davenport, their daughter

The Mallinson Family
Arthur (Julien St. Juste) Mallinson, Earl Carfax, former agent for hire
Katelina (Kitty) Velasquez Mallinson, Countess Carfax, his wife, former British and Spanish intelligence agent
Leo Ashford, her son
Timothy Ashford, her son
Guenevere (Genny) Ashford, Kitty and Julien's daughter

Hubert Mallinson, spymaster, Julien's uncle
Amelia Mallinson, his wife
Lucinda Mallinson, their youngest daughter

David Mallinson, MP, Hubert and Amelia's son
Simon Tanner, playwright, his lover
Amy Craven, their ward
Jamie Craven, their ward

Others

Alexander (Sandy) Trenor

Elizabeth (Bet) Simcox, his mistress
Nan Simcox Lucan, her sister
Sam Lucan, Nan's husband
Robert (Robby) Simcox, Bet and Nan's brother
Lady Marchmain, Sandy's mother
Lord Marchmain, Sandy's father

Allston, Sandy's friend
Lavering, Sandy's friend
Sallie (or Susie), Lavering's mistress

George Dawkins
Tom McCandless

Frederick Talbot, Marquis of Glenister, Malcolm's godfather, Elsinore League member
Lady Shroppington, Elsinore League member

*Arthur Wellesley, Duke of Wellington
*Emily Harriet Somerset, his niece
*Fitzroy Somerset, her husband, Wellington's secretary
*Charlotte Somerset, their daughter

*Henry Brougham, MP, Queen Caroline's lawyer

*Sir Nathaniel Conant, Chief Magistrate of Bow Street
*Lord Sidmouth, Home Secretary
*Lord Castlereagh, Foreign Secretary
*Lord Liverpool, Prime Minister

John Bennet, hotel proprietor
Anne Elliot, his daughter

Jeremy Roth, Bow Street runner

What's mine is yours, and what's yours is mine.
—Shakespeare, *Measure for Measure,* Act V, scene i

CHAPTER 1

London
October 1820

The smell washed over her as she stepped over the threshold of the Green Dragon. Sour ale. Pungent wine. Gin. Tallow candles. Cheap scent masking stale sweat. The smell of home. Or what had once been home. It was sharper than she remembered. Or perhaps it was her senses that had changed.

The floor seemed to have sagged. The uneven boards poked against her feet. Or perhaps that was the kid soles of her half boots, softer than anything she'd worn in the old days. Bet picked her way through the crowd, looking for familiar faces. Jack Watkins, whom she'd played tagg with when they were five, shared her first kiss with when they were eleven, and more when they were fourteen, glanced right past her. Jenny Green, who had been both a friend and a competitor for clients, stared at her for a moment, opened her mouth as though to speak, then shook her head and looked away.

"Can I get you anything, miss?"

It was a waiter who had started less than a month before Bet left St. Giles to move in with Sandy. Tim, she thought his name was. She smiled in greeting. His gaze flickered over her face, and for a moment she thought he recognized her. Then he shook his head. "Sorry, miss. You remind me of someone I used know. Begging your pardon, but this isn't the best place for a lady. Do you need help finding a hackney?"

"No. Thank you. I'm meeting someone."

Confusion and uncertainty flickered across his gaze, as though he was revising his first impression of her. "If you're in trouble—"

Funny how a well-cut pelisse, an elegant bonnet, and a better accent could bring on protective instincts. No one had ever worried much about her in the old days. Those who paid attention to her at all assumed she could take care of herself. Which she had done. But if anything, she was stronger now.

"I'll be fine," Bet said in a firm voice. Though it was odd to realize the one place that had been home wasn't home anymore. Because Sandy's flat in the Albany could never really be her home.

Another waiter, whom she didn't remember, came over to her. "The gentleman is upstairs."

Tim cast a worried look at her. Bet smiled at him and followed the second waiter from the taproom. She lifted the skirt of her sapphire blue silk pelisse as she reached the stairs. The boards creaked and sagged. When she put a hand on the stair rail, the splintery wood scraped through her doeskin glove. Up the stairs she had often climbed with a gentleman or to meet a gentleman. Funny, she'd been quite matter-of-fact about that sort of encounter. Wary, because one never quite knew what one was getting into, but it had been her life and she'd made the best of it. Until Sandy. After Sandy it had grown difficult to think of anyone else in that way. Though she might have to when—

Bet resolutely shut her mind to the future as the waiter indicated one of the doors off the landing. She nodded and opened the door. With more trepidation than she had felt going to any past encounter here. After all, with those sorts of

2

encounters, at least one knew more or less what to expect. She wasn't even sure quite whom she was meeting, save that the message had made it imperative she keep the appointment.

She opened the door. The room was in shadow, lit only by a single lamp on a table across from the door. The smell of brandy, much finer than that generally served at the Green Dragon, wafted towards her. Until she'd met Sandy, she hadn't known that smell. The man sitting in a chair by the table with the lamp got to his feet at her entrance. That was unexpected.

"Miss Simcox." That was unexpected too. At the Green Dragon, she was Bet, not Miss Simcox. "Thank you for coming."

He spoke in the accents of Sandy's world, Eton or Harrow, Oxford or Cambridge, Brooks's or White's. He wasn't a tall man, but he radiated power. His gray-streaked hair might be brown or dark blond. The lamplight picked out sharp, imperious features. He looked to be in his late fifties.

She closed the door. "From the tone of your letter, I didn't have a great deal of choice."

"One always has a choice, though sometimes one or more of the options seem untenable. May I pour you some brandy? I brought it with me."

"Thank you." Somehow accepting the drink put them on the same level. And she could use it.

She sat in the chair on the other side of the small table with the lamp and the bottle of brandy and pulled off her gloves. The stair rail had left dark smears on them.

He poured a glass of brandy and set it on the table beside her. "I see no sense in prevaricating. Do you know who I am?"

"I don't believe we've ever met." She made it not quite a question. Dear God. He wasn't someone she'd spent the night with, was he? She'd have sworn not. But could she really be sure she'd recognize all of them?

"No, you're quite right. We haven't met. My tastes never ran to

St. Giles." He took a deliberate drink of brandy and set his glass beside her own. "But I'm your lover's father."

The world spun, though she hadn't taken a sip of the brandy. Sandy still thought of Lord Marchmain as his father. But Bet knew, because Sandy had told her, that in pure biology Sandy's father was Alistair Rannoch. Who supposedly had died over three years ago, in a carriage accident that may not have been an accident.

"That's generally the response of people I've revealed myself to recently." The gentleman sank back in his chair. "Suffice it to say, I had my reasons for disappearing. And believe me, I don't reveal myself lightly."

Bet pulled her second glove from her fingertips. Her gaze locked on the black stitching on the pale gray. As though somehow the neat stitches held a code that would explain this confusing world she had stumbled into. "So you must have your reasons for wanting to talk to me."

"I generally have reasons for what I do." He took a sip of brandy. "I want to see my son."

Bet's gaze locked on that of the man across the candle from her. His eyes might be blue or green or gray. They were hard as agate. "Sandy doesn't think of himself as your son."

"No, I don't imagine he does. He doesn't know me at all. Which is all the more reason for me to get to know him."

"Why?" Bet asked before she could think better of it. "Why now? You've known you were his father since he was born."

"True enough. But it's not the sort of thing one reveals to a child. At least, not unless one is my putative son, Malcolm Rannoch, who does things in ways few others would. Sandy is no longer a child. And my own circumstances have changed."

"If you want to talk to Sandy, you should reach out to him." That was true, though perhaps a mistake to put into words. "I don't see where I come into it."

Alistair Rannoch twisted the stem of his glass between his

fingers. "I think you underrate yourself, Miss Simcox. You obviously mean a great deal to Alexander." He ran his gaze over her. A polite gaze, but it seemed to slice through her silk pelisse and the sarcenet gown beneath and even the laces of her stays and her muslin chemise more effectively than the sharpest knife. "I'm sure you have ways of persuading Sandy. Just as you do other gentlemen."

Bet lifted her chin. "I don't need to try to persuade Sandy of anything. And there haven't been any other gentlemen for a long time."

He sat back in his chair and regarded her, glass held between two fingers. "No, I don't suppose you've needed anyone else since he's been keeping you."

"Sandy and I are—"

"Yes?"

Bet gripped her hands in her lap, fingers tight round her gloves. "It's none of your affair."

Mr. Rannoch inclined his head. "You're fond of him. That helps. I'm sure you want what's best for him."

That was the sort of thing Sandy's parents said. Or at least that she assumed they said. She'd scarcely spoken to either of them except for one disastrous meeting at the Carfax ball last June, which had mostly involved Lady Marchmain's hurling insults while Bet and Lord Marchmain tried to separate Sandy and his mother. "I don't think Sandy's and my relationship is any concern of yours."

"I'll admit I haven't been a conventional father, but a son's domestic arrangements can't but be a father's concern."

Bet reached for her glass and took a deliberate drink of brandy. "Then you should ask Sandy."

Alistair Rannoch swirled the brandy in his glass. "In addition to wanting what's best for Sandy, I assume you want what's best for your brother."

Bet's fingers bit into her glass. "Of course I want what's best for Robby." And her brother Robby's future (as in his safety in the next week, or even the next hour) had frequently been a source of concern, even after she moved in with Sandy. But Robby was now employed as a groom to the new Lord Carfax and doing very well in his position, so no longer quite such a frequent source of concern to Bet and her sister Nan.

Mr. Rannoch took a sip of brandy. "You must have been pleased when Carfax took him on."

"We have a number of reasons to be grateful to Lord Carfax." Still so odd to use that name for a man she had once called Mr. St. Juste, and now improbably addressed as Julien, for he told her couldn't abide being called Carfax.

"Yes, you have powerful friends, but I don't know that they'll be able to help you now." Alistair Rannoch returned his glass to the table. "I am desolate to be the bearer of bad news, Miss Simcox, but your brother is presently under arrest at the Bow Street Public Office."

Bet's glass tilted in her fingers. "At the—"

"Unless he's already been taken to Newgate."

Panic closed round her throat. The fear of arrest had been a commonplace part of her life growing up. Her father had been arrested for stealing a pocket watch when she was six. He'd been hanged five days before her seventh birthday. But Robby was too clever for thievery now. Julien—Lord Carfax—paid him well. And Robby was intensely loyal to Julien. "He wouldn't—"

"Difficult to know what anyone would or wouldn't do, I find. But as it happens, he didn't steal. He fired a pistol at the Duke of Wellington."

The knot round her throat tightened. That should be even more incredible. But—

Alistair Rannoch held her gaze, his own as cold and lethal as a knife blade. "At the duke's carriage, I should say. The unrest in London is an epidemic these days. Perhaps not surprising your brother was caught up in it."

6

London had been at a fever pitch since the summer over the new King George IV's efforts to divorce his long-estranged wife, Queen Caroline. Most common folk were (quite sensibly, in Bet's opinion) on the queen's side. There had been demonstrations outside Parliament, where the trial was taking place in the House of Lords, and demonstrations outside of the houses of many prominent noblemen in the government, such as Wellington. The trial was about to resume with the queen's defense. Robby had worn a white cockade in support of the queen for months and had gone to several demonstrations, Bet knew. But he didn't even own a pistol. "If the duke—"

"Wellington is unharmed. But the bullet struck a bystander, who is under a doctor's care."

Her stomach lurched. "If there was a crowd, they can't know Robby did it."

"No, that's true." Alistair Rannoch lifted his glass and took a slow drink of brandy. "But the case against him is strong. It would take considerable influence to get it dismissed."

Bet drew in and released her breath, willing the tightness in her throat to relax enough that she could say what needed to be said. "What do you want me to do?"

7

CHAPTER 2

*M*élanie Rannoch set down her pencil. "That helps. I think the scene between Ginette and Nick still drags on too long. But we need all the information."

Simon Tanner leaned over the rehearsal table to look at the script of Mélanie's latest play. They had stayed to go over it after a read-through with some of the actors in the Tavistock company. Simon was a part owner of the Tavistock Theatre and a playwright himself. He'd also become one of Mélanie's closest friends since she'd left all she had known and come to the alien world of the British beau monde with her husband. "What if you moved the discussion about Nick's past to the end? I've been thinking Ginette and Nick need another scene in Act III in any case."

"Of course." The pieces of the story reformed in Mélanie's mind, like cards with plot points. Or fragments of evidence in an investigation. "And then the tension of exactly what Ginette is thinking about it hangs over the whole play. Simon, that's brilliant."

Simon grinned. "Just shifting your brilliant words about."

The boards of the stage creaked as Mélanie's children, Colin and Jessica, played hide and seek in the wings with Amy and Jamie

Craven, the younger of Simon's four wards. And then there was another creak from the front of the house, and the patter of feet. Mélanie tensed at the memory of the body she and the children had discovered in the wings of the Tavistock less than a year ago.

The footsteps pounded closer. A cloaked figure ran down the aisle.

"Mélanie." Nan Lucan stopped at the edge of the stage, breathing hard, the hood of her cherry red cloak thrown back, her curly dark hair slipping from its pins and falling round her face. "Robby's been arrested."

Mélanie sprang to her feet.

"Is he in the Tower?" Jessica ran to the edge of the stage.

"Probably Newgate." Colin wrapped his arms round his little sister before she could tumble into the pit.

"Not yet." Nan gripped the edge of the stage and boosted herself up. "I think he's still at Bow Street."

"With Uncle Jeremy?" Colin asked.

"I don't know." Nan's hands slipped on the wood.

Simon ran forwards and helped her up onto the stage. "What's the charge?"

"Shooting. At the Duke of Wellington's carriage." Nan's gaze shot to Simon, scouring his face for answers to an unspoken question.

Simon bent to scoop up four-year-old Jamie, who had hurtled into his knees. "Robby's come to some Leveller meetings." The Levellers were a group dedicated to reform that centered round the theatre, and they were firmly behind Queen Caroline. "But however we may skirt the law, we don't advocate violence. And I haven't heard Robby give any indication that he does."

"He's been set up," Nan said. "But even if he hasn't—"

Mélanie tightened her arms round her children, who had run to her side. "We have to get him out."

～

9

MALCOLM RANNOCH TOOK a drink of wine and turned over the last of the papers on the table before him. "It's a good speech, Henry."

Henry Brougham picked up the decanter of Bordeaux and refilled their glasses. "It needs to be better than good. It needs to be the most bloody brilliant speech I've ever given. And yes, I have a healthy respect for my own speeches."

"You could feel the restlessness in the chamber by the time the prosecution wrapped up." Julien Mallinson, whom Malcom could still not quite get used to remembering was Lord Carfax and therefore one of those presiding over the queen's trial, scanned the first page of the speech again. "It was quite entertaining watching you shred prosecution witnesses to bits. Even some Tories are calling the prosecution's witness the *non mi ricordos.* Much of the king's case is already discredited."

"Much, not all." Brougham leaned forwards, shirtsleeved elbows on the polished cherrywood of the table. His coat dangled by one shoulder over the chair behind him. "We still don't have the votes. There are more Tories in Parliament than Whigs. It comes down to politics in the end. My case has to be good enough to give enough Tories cover to vote with us. They've got to feel they'd be fools to see the situation any way but in the queen's favor." He tossed down a drink of Bordeaux. "Take a pen to it."

Malcolm looked back at the draft speech. He too was in his shirtsleeves, as was Julien. The three of them had been closeted in the sitting room at Brooks's for over an hour. "I'm not a barrister."

"I need another eye. And you're the only one of my colleagues who may possibly write better than I do."

Malcolm reached for his glass, gaze on the speech. "That's mostly Mélanie."

Julien slouched back in his chair. "Mélanie's a brilliant writer, but you're not bad yourself, Malcolm."

"And together you're a force to be reckoned with." Brougham frowned. "Why isn't Mélanie here?"

"We're at Brooks's," Malcolm pointed out.

"That's a point." Brougham stretched out his legs. "Stupid club conventions. We should meet in Berkeley Square."

"She's at the Tavistock," Malcolm said. "Plays don't stop premiering just because Parliament and the royal family and the British populace are turned on their heads."

Brougham nudged the speech closer to Malcolm with the edge of his glass. "Take it home and see how the two of you can sharpen it."

Malcolm took the papers and folded them. Brougham was set to open the queen's defense on charges of carrying on "a most unbecoming and disgusting intimacy" with her courier Bartolomeo Bergami. As Julien said, Brougham had done an able job cross-examining during the prosecution's case, but as Brougham had pointed out, they still did not have the votes. The Tories, the governing party, were backing the king, largely out of self-preservation to stay in power. The Whigs were backing the queen for the reverse reason. Many of them believed in her constitutional rights, but they also had hopes of bringing down the Tory government. And Brougham, a noted Radical, was leading the charge. Because it could further his ambitions, personally and in terms of what he could achieve for reform. And just possibly also because he cared about the queen. "We'll see what we can do."

Brougham nodded. "Thank you." The ring in his voice was heartfelt. "If—"

The door opened to admit one of the Brooks's footmen. "Forgive me, Lord Carfax. Mr. Rannoch. Mr. Brougham. There's a gentleman—"

"I need to see Carfax. And Rannoch." A broad-shouldered man pushed past the footman.

It was Sam Lucan, former gun dealer who had worked with Mélanie in the Peninsula. And then turned broker of various mostly illegal things in St. Giles. He was now semi-legitimate and also a good friend. "I need your help." Sam looked from Julien to Malcolm without even glancing at Brougham. "Robby's been arrested."

"What?" Julien pushed back his chair, nearly toppling it onto the Axminster rug. Robby Simcox, whose sister Nan was married to Sam, was in his employ as a groom.

Malcolm nodded at the footman to withdraw. "Why?"

"Shooting at the Duke of Wellington, they say."

"Oh, for God's sake," Julien said.

Brougham pushed himself to his feet. "Simcox was protesting?"

"Well, yes. Robby doesn't like what the duke stands for—"

"No argument there from me," Brougham said.

"But he wouldn't shoot a gun at him."

"No, Robby's too sensible to shoot at anyone these days," Julien said.

"Wellington's been damned intractable lately," Brougham said. "I can imagine someone shooting at him. There are moments— quite a few of them, actually—when I'd find myself more than in sympathy with someone who wanted to shoot at him." He glanced at Malcolm. "Sorry."

"Is the duke all right?" Malcolm asked. He had worked with Wellington in the Peninsula, during the Waterloo campaign, and in Paris after Waterloo, as a diplomat and an intelligence agent. He and the duke were poles apart politically, but he liked Wellington. Mélanie would claim he'd never entirely get past his loyalty to the duke. Malcolm wasn't sure he agreed, but he certainly wished no harm on Wellington. Or on anyone.

"He wasn't hit," Sam said. "But the bullet struck someone else. Not sure of the name. He's with a doctor. And God yes, I'm sorry, for the man, but a doctor's seeing to him. Now we need someone to make sure Robby doesn't hang."

"He won't." Julien grabbed his coat from the back of his chair.

Malcolm reached for his own coat. "I'll go to Bow Street. Brougham—"

"Go," Brougham said. "I'm a lawyer. I know when a case is urgent."

⁓

BET STARED AT ALISTAIR RANNOCH. Sandy's father. The man who seemingly held her brother's fate in his hands. "What do you want me to do?"

Alistair Rannoch sat back in his chair, as though it were the sort of leather arm chair that she imagined men like him lounged in in clubs instead of straight-backed wood with cracked slats, and took a sip of brandy. "Merely what we both know you're going to have to do sooner or later in any case. Leave Alexander to get on with his life."

She should have seen it coming. A part of her had seen it coming from the moment he first tried to blackmail her. Her fingers tightened round her own glass. "If it's inevitable, why go to such lengths?"

"Alexander's a romantic. He'll drag it out."

"You don't know him." Her voice came out sharper than she intended.

"Just because I haven't hovered over him the way Raoul O'Roarke has over Malcolm doesn't mean I haven't had reports on him all his life."

A chill cut through her. Strange that anything else could be frightening beside the threat to Robby, but the thought of this man, who she hadn't known had any connection to Sandy until little over a year ago, whom Sandy hadn't known he had a connection to himself, watching over Sandy and getting reports on him cut like icy air in winter when one couldn't afford coal.

Alistair Rannoch picked up the bottle and refilled both their glasses. "If he drags his feet he'll miss out on opportunities in life."

"What sort of opportunities?"

"My dear Miss Simcox. You can hardly expect me to confide in

13

you. But if you want what's best for Alexander and your brother, you'll do as I ask. I can make sure you don't want for creature comforts."

"Do you think I care—"

"I do you the credit of thinking you're hardheaded enough to have a care for your future. Sandy may have delusions about the future—or more likely ignore it entirely—but surely you are too sensible to see anything lasting in a relationship that wouldn't thrive in the most romanticized novel. You must know it's only a matter of time before this ends. End it now and I can protect your brother and see to it neither of you wants for anything."

"How can you protect Robby if he's been arrested?"

"I may be presumed dead, but I can still bring influence to bear. It would be enough to get your brother released."

"Or to keep him imprisoned."

"As you say."

Bet forced her glass to her lips and took a swallow. It burned a trail down her throat. "Are you saying you'll do all that if I simply give you my word I'll leave Sandy?"

"My dear Miss Simcox. I rarely do anything based on anyone's word. Even that of a fellow gentleman."

"So you'll hardly take mine. What then?"

Alistair Rannoch folded his arms across his chest. "I have great faith in your ingenuity, Miss Simcox. Surely you can find a way to make your decision clear to Sandy. And to me."

CHAPTER 3

*M*alcolm scanned the Brown Bear tavern as he and Julien stepped over the threshold. Hopkins, one of the patrols, had told them Jeremy Roth was at the Brown Bear and that Robby Simcox was being held upstairs. The Brown Bear served almost as an extension of the Bow Street Public Office.

He caught sight of Roth in the shadows on the far side of the tavern, at a table, long legs stretched out, shoulders hunched as he bent over his notebook.

"Thank God you're here," Malcolm said, when he and Julien had picked their way across the room.

Roth pushed himself to his feet. "I was about to send to Berkeley Square. I've only just got the details. I'm not the one who brought him in."

"How bad is the case?" Julien asked, dragging out a chair as they all sat round the table.

"He was found near the pistol, and several witnesses have informed against him. But a lot of it's circumstantial." Roth cast a glance round. A number of men Malcolm recognized as runners and patrols were huddled at other tables. "Everyone's on edge right now with the trial and the protests. Wellington's involved.

Obviously they want to find someone to punish and to be able to say we've got the perpetrator in custody. But it's more than that." Roth leaned forwards, his voice a rough whisper. "Pressure's been brought to bear. To arrest Simcox and to pursue the case against him."

"From whom?" Malcolm asked.

"I don't know." Roth's mouth tightened. "I haven't been able to discover it."

"Simcox was set up," Julien said.

Roth regarded him in the flickering lamplight. "You seem very sure."

"I am. I know him. And yes, I know a number of people capable of all sorts of criminal acts. Simcox wouldn't do this. Whatever your opinion of me, I'm a reasonable judge of character."

Roth gave a faint grin. "I have an excellent opinion of you, Carfax."

"God, can't you call me Julien?"

"When my superiors aren't present to look askance at me." Roth flipped a page in his notebook. "I understand Simcox had been to protests before."

"Yes, I know he had. He talked quite freely about it. Half London have done the same."

"People can do things in a crowd they'd never do on their own," Roth said. "I saw that in battle."

"But the crowd weren't firing pistols," Julien said. "It's rare for anyone in London to fire a pistol in the general run of things. And Simcox doesn't have a pistol."

"Could he have stolen it from you?"

"We only have one in the house, and I keep it locked up. We have young children. I'm sure you appreciate that."

"Quite," said Roth, who had children himself. "But there are any number of other ways he could have acquired a weapon. I know he used to associate with quite a different crowd in St. Giles."

"Whose side are you on?" Julien demanded.

"I'm trying to explore all the options. And see if I can pick apart the case against him by defending it."

Julien inclined his head. "Start with your opponent's perspective. Good spycraft."

"Who are the witnesses?" Malcolm asked.

Roth flipped to another page. "An assortment of those in the crowd. One of the Apsley House footmen. They seem solid on the surface, but all sorts of people can be paid to say all sorts of things. And Lady Fitzroy Somerset."

"Harriet was in the carriage?" Malcolm asked. Harriet Somerset, Wellington's neice, was married to Fitzroy Somerset, who had been the duke's secretary since the Peninsula and was a good friend of Malcolm's.

"She and Fitzroy Somerset and their daughter were in the carriage with the duke," Roth said. "I understand the little girl is—"

"Five," Malcolm said. "She was born right before Waterloo. They're all right?"

"Just shaken."

"God," Julien said, with the feeling of a father. "What did they see?"

"The duke and Somerset were facing away. Lady Fitzroy describes a blur of movement. My colleagues didn't try to speak with the little girl."

"Perhaps we should if she's not too shaken," Julien said. "Children can have a keen eye for detail. Mine notice things that slip even my eye and Kitty's."

"Is Wellington pushing for Robby's arrest?" Malcolm asked.

"Not excessively, that I can tell," Roth said. "He mainly seemed concerned for his niece and great-niece. I understand he's at Apsley House with them. If he wanted to apply pressure for arrest, he could do so openly. Pressure from him would have more force openly exerted, in the circumstances. So I can only assume it's coming from other quarters."

"Possibly because Robby works for me," Julien said.

"You have enemies," Roth conceded.

"What about the man who was shot?" Malcolm asked.

Roth flipped to another page in the notebook. "A John Bennet. Owns a hotel in Bloomsbury apparently. Poor devil was in the wrong place at the wrong time."

"How bad is he?" Julien asked.

"The bullet passed through his shoulder and he hit his head when he fell. But he's expected to recover."

"Thank God for that." Julien pushed his chair back. "We want to see Robby."

"Of course."

Roth took them upstairs to a small, low-ceilinged room that the runners often used to temporarily hold prisoners. Laura, who was now Malcolm's stepmother, had been held in this same room in the days when she was Colin and Jessica's governess and had been accused of murder. Not a pleasant memory, though at least Laura had been cleared.

Roth unlocked the door to reveal Robby Simcox, sitting bolt upright on a straight-backed chair. He pushed himself to his feet at their entrance. His thick fair hair was disordered, as though he'd been digging his fingers into it. His gaze shot from Julien to Malcolm, blue eyes dark with pent-up concern. "I didn't do it."

"I didn't for a minute think you had." Julien crossed the room and touched Robby's shoulder in a way Malcolm would have found unthinkable a year and a half ago when he'd thought of Julien as a cold-blooded agent. It wasn't quite so surprising now he was used to Julien as a father.

"I'll leave you to talk," Roth said. "I'm trying to persuade Sampson to let me take over the case."

Julien pushed Robby back into the chair. He and Malcolm sat

on the edge of the bed. "What happened?" Julien asked in a soft voice.

"It was after I got the horses stabled. I went along to the Rose & Garter to meet some mates. It was—"

"Your evening off. Quite."

"And we got to talking about the trial starting up again, and someone said we shouldn't just be sitting drinking and complaining, and the next thing I knew we were walking towards the Grosvenor Gate. I didn't even realize we were heading towards Apsley House until we were standing in front. There was a crowd already there, shouting at the carriages that came by, going to or from Grosvenor Street. Assuming anyone in a fine carriage was on the king's side. Which is nonsense, if they'd only think. I mean, nearly half Parliament supports the queen, and I could tell them Whigs have just as fine carriages as Tories. Finer." He gave a faint grin.

"And much abler grooms," Julien said. "What happened next?"

The grin faded. Robby scraped the toe of his boot over the floor boards. "It wasn't the first time I've gone to a protest."

"No, I know," Julien said. "Difficult to avoid them in London these past months. And plenty of cause to protest. I've gone to more than one myself."

Robby's eyes widened. "You have?"

"I'm fortunate enough to have a voice in Parliament. That doesn't mean I don't try to find other ways to be heard. And that I don't have an interest in what's being said. If the rest of those in the Lords listened a bit, they might find fewer protesters yelling at their carriages."

Robby stared at Julien for a moment. "You always were a rum cove."

"I've gone with him," Malcolm said.

Robby's gaze shot to Malcolm. "You're an MP. You don't need to protest to be heard."

"It's one way to bring about change," Malcolm said. "It doesn't always work, but it gets attention."

Robby shook his head. "Bet's always saying the gentry are different, but I don't think this is what she meant. In any case, suddenly a new carriage came by, but it slowed down. I heard someone shout it was the duke, and in truth I wasn't sure which duke they meant. One of the royal ones, I thought, which was stupid because we were at Apsley House, but I wasn't thinking. The crowd pressed tighter and there was pushing and shoving and the next thing I knew I heard a pistol go off. Then someone backed right into me, and I fell on top of a bunch of other blokes. I was trying to get up when people started yelling 'There he is,' and when I reached out to push myself up on the pavement, my hand touched a pistol." Robby looked from Julien to Malcolm. "I'd never seen it before, I swear. I didn't even have a pistol when you hired me to protect Lumley, sir. Why would I have taken one to a protest? Why would I have shot at Wellington? I mean, whatever his politics now, he beat Boney."

Malcolm's wife and father might have interesting things to say about that last, though whatever their opinion of the outcome of Waterloo, Malcolm was quite sure neither of them would ever have attacked Wellington either. Not unless it was on the battle-field. Where his father had fought against the duke, if not face to face.

"I looked round to see whose pistol it was," Robby continued. "And someone said 'Him, he's the one, he's holding the pistol.' Which I wasn't. I only touched it, but then of course I froze. Next thing I knew two men grabbed me. I almost fought back, but I knew I couldn't get away."

"Sensible," Julien said.

"Wouldn't have thought you'd say so, sir."

"Even I know the risk of fighting when outnumbered."

"You just wouldn't have admitted you were outnumbered."

"In a crowd I might. I've always had a healthier sense of self-preservation than I let people think."

"Well, I just kept saying 'It wasn't me,' and others started pushing and someone said 'He's hit.'" Robby looked from Julien to Malcolm. "Do you know what happened to him? Not the duke, the man who was shot, I mean?"

"He's alive," Malcolm said. "And not in danger, from what we understand."

"Thank God for that." Robby scraped a hand over his face. "I don't even know his name."

"Bennet," Julien said. "A hotel owner who was in the wrong place at the wrong time."

"He must have gone to protest too."

"People from all walks of life have been protesting," Malcolm said.

"And one of them shot off the pistol."

"Someone who was there did," Julien agreed. "It may have been someone hired for the job."

"Shooting at the duke?"

"It seems so," Malcolm said. "Sam's gone to talk to Raoul. They both have sources who might know about someone's being hired for a job like this. Did you recognize anyone near you when the pistol went off?"

Robby shook his head. "I'd been separated from my friends. The crowd was so tight all I remember seeing were backs and waistcoats and elbows. Truth to tell, I was just trying to keep myself upright and get out of the crowd." He looked between them again. "It's bad, isn't it? No one's going to believe me."

Julien leaned forwards and put a hand on Robby's shoulder. "We do. And we're rather formidable when we put our minds to something. Especially when our wives do so as well."

CHAPTER 4

"*Y*ou can't play that card." Leo Ashford leaned over the baize-covered table to look at the card his brother Timothy had just set down.

"Can too," Timothy declared.

"It's very clever, Timothy." Kitty Mallinson shifted two-year-old Genny in her lap as Genny turned the pages of a cloth book. "But Leo's right that it's not strictly within the rules."

"Why do we have to play by the rules?" Timothy asked. "Daddy says you make your own rules in life."

Kitty could hear her husband saying just that. Julien was an excellent influence on the boys. Timothy had started calling him Daddy not too long after Kitty and Julien's marriage in January. Leo now often did as well.

"Not in the middle of a game when we started with one set of rules," Leo said.

Timothy leaned forwards. "Life's a game. Daddy says that too."

"He also says life isn't fair," Kitty said. "But that doesn't mean a game has to be if we're setting the rules. Daddy would agree. He believes in fairness." Even though Julien had played a particularly vicious spy game himself. But perhaps all the more reason he had come to believe one could be fair in one's dealings with others. Kitty had herself, though she wasn't quite sure when. Perhaps round the same time she had admitted she trusted Julien enough to marry him.

Timothy frowned. "I think we should have different rules next time."

"As long as you start with rules everyone agrees on that seem reasonable." Kitty grabbed the cloth book before Genny could drop it and tumble off her lap after it.

"I'll get Daddy to help me come up with the rules," Timothy said.

"Right now, let's finish this game," Leo said. "With these rules."

Timothy scowled and put his elbows on the table to study his cards. "All right, as long as you—"

He broke off as the door opened to admit Albert, one of the footmen. "Miss Simcox has called, my lady."

"Show her in," Kitty said.

For Bet to call on her own in the evening was surprising but not wholly unusual. The children greeted her with cries of delight. Genny scrambled off Kitty's lap to fling her arms round Bet's knees.

Bet scooped up Genny and hugged her and smiled at the boys, but her gaze went to Kitty, wide with anxiety. Kitty pushed herself to her feet.

"Is Julien here?" Bet asked.

"No, he's at Brooks's with Malcolm and Henry Brougham," Kitty said. "Can I help?" She glanced at the boys. "Perhaps we should go into the study? While the boys finish their game?"

Easy enough to leave the study door ajar while the boys returned to their game. Genny toddled along after Kitty and Bet, holding Bet's hand, but she was too young to understand whatever Bet quite obviously needed to discuss. Kitty poured two glasses of Rannoch malt and gave one to Bet. "What's happened?"

Bet took a quick drink of whisky, glanced at Genny, who had

23

plopped down on the hearth rug, and looked back at Kitty. "Robby's been arrested."

Kitty's gaze jerked to the back of the house, towards the mews and the stables. "It's his night off—"

"He went to a protest. Apparently he was arrested for shooting at the Duke of Wellington's carriage."

Kitty nearly dropped her own glass. "The duke—"

"He's all right. But a bystander was wounded."

"Who told you?"

Bet took another sip of whisky. "Alistair Rannoch." Her gaze raked Kitty's face. "Did you know he was alive?"

Kitty took a drink from her own glass. "Yes. But only for a matter of days. Does Sandy know?"

"Not yet. Not that I know, at least. I came straight from Mr. Rannoch." Bet hunched her shoulders, fingers curled tight round her glass.

"Bet." Kitty pressed her into one of the two chairs in front of the desk and drew the other chair up beside her. "Did Mr. Rannoch threaten to harm your brother?"

Fear shot across Bet's face, followed by grim certainty. "Robby's already facing harm. How many people like him are brought up on charges and acquitted?"

Kitty had lost her parents young, had grown up in the midst of a war, had bartered her body for information before she quite understood the consequences. But her life had been soft and easy compared to the life Bet had had as a girl. She leaned forwards and squeezed Bet's cold hand. "Mr. Rannoch offered to intervene if you did as he asked?"

"Yes." Bet's fingers were numb in Kitty's own.

"What did he want?"

"What do you think? For me to leave Sandy." Bet jerked her hand to her lips and took a drink of whisky.

"Rather crude for Alistair Rannoch," Kitty said. "I'd say it shows desperation."

Bet took another drink of whisky. "I'm thinking I should do as he asks."

"Bet, no." Kitty's fingers tightened round her own glass. "You've got Julien and the Rannochs. And me. And the O'Roarkes and the Davenports. We can stop Mr. Rannoch and protect your brother."

"Maybe." Bet's gaze locked on Kitty's own, level and direct. "I don't discount what you all can do. I'm more grateful to all of you than I can say. But you can't be sure. You can't know what you'll be risking yourselves."

"We run risks every day."

Bet cast a glance at Genny on the hearth rug. "And you weigh the consequences."

"This is certainly worth the risk."

"Is it? For me to stay with Sandy a few more months? Even a year? Because we all know how this is going to end. Even when I'm dining at your table or dancing at your ball where some people look askance at me and the rest of you politely pretend I'm something I'm not, we all know how this is going to end. I never imagined it could go on this long. I know I've been selfish—"

"Bet, don't be silly. You're in love with Sandy."

Bet's shoulders hunched inwards. "Well, of course."

"And Sandy's in love with you."

"Sandy may think he is. But he can't—it can't last. He knows it, and I know it, and all our polite friends know it. It's going to hurt like the devil for it to end, but I have to go through it at some point, so why not now when I can make sure my brother is safe?"

"Because it's wrong."

"I always took you for a pragmatist, Lady—Kitty."

As she had always considered herself to be one. "A pragmatist knows to hold on to what matters in life." Kitty bent down to scoop up Genny, who had toddled into her chair. "I once thought Julien was bound to leave me. I sometimes wondered if I should leave him first, before I could be hurt more." She'd actually lain awake in bed beside him, thinking it. And then turned her head on the pillow to look at his face and known she couldn't.

Bet gave a twisted smile. "It's different for you. Oh, I know the challenges you've faced, and I admire you for getting past them. For fighting for the person you love. But you and Julien are from the same world."

Kitty opened her mouth to argue, just as Genny grabbed her jade beads.

"It may not seem like it to you, but from St. Giles your world and Julien's are two peas in a pod."

Kitty detached Genny's hand from the beads and pulled a comb from her hair for her daughter to play with. "When we married, Julien thought his uncle would stop it."

"But he didn't. Even if he'd tried, the polite world wouldn't have looked askance at your marrying."

"Bet—you can't give way, because it's letting Alistair Rannoch win."

"I don't have the luxury of thinking about that."

"And because you can't trust Alistair Rannoch." Kitty tossed down a drink of whisky and pushed herself to her feet, holding Genny. "We're going to Bow Street."

NAN PAUSED in the glow of the lantern outside the Brown Bear, fingers tight on her gown as she held it up to avoid the muck in the street. She and Mélanie had walked the relatively short distance from the Tavistock while Simon took Colin and Jessica home to Berkeley Square.

"It's all right," Mélanie said, as Nan stared at the door as though it might bite. "It's not even Bow Street, it's a tavern."

"A tavern full of runners."

"That's why we're here. It's probably where they're holding Robby."

"That's supposed to make me feel better?"

"No, but it rather necessitates our going in."

Mélanie opened the door and stepped into the common room, drawing Nan with her. Thank God, there was Jeremy Roth across the room. He caught her gaze and came towards her and Nan. "Malcolm and Julien are upstairs with Simcox. With your brother, Mrs. Lucan."

"How is he?" Nan's concern for her brother triumphed over the fear of being surrounded by Bow Street runners and patrols.

"He's unhurt. He's been very cooperative. That's good for him."

"Is anything in this bloody mess good for him?" Nan demanded.

"Some things are better than others. If—" Roth broke off as the door thudded open again. Mélanie looked over her shoulder to see Bet hurry in, followed by Kitty. Bet ran across the room to them, heedless of the looks from those at other tables, impatience getting the better of her usual care.

"He's all right, Miss Simcox," Roth said quickly. "I can take you and your sister up to see him."

"But he's under arrest."

"At present. Yes. Malcolm and Julien are with him."

Mélanie and Kitty stayed in the common room to give Nan and Bet time with their brother. Mélanie was eager to hear what Robby had to say, but Malcolm would give them a report. She got pints of stout for herself and Kitty, deciding they both could use it, and they settled at the table in the corner where Roth had been sitting.

Kitty took a long drink of stout. "Thank you. I needed fortification."

"Bet came to Carfax House?" Mélanie asked. "How did she learn about Robby?"

"Alistair Rannoch told her."

Mélanie froze, her tankard halfway to her lips. "Christ. We didn't think he'd act quite so soon."

"He told her he'll help Robby if she agrees to leave Sandy."

Mélanie set her tankard down with shaking fingers. "I have the horrible feeling we've been outplayed."

"Of all the moves Alistair Rannoch might have made, I don't see how we could have predicted this one." Kitty undid the ties on her cloak and tossed it over the chair back. "Mélanie—we can't let her do this. She told me she might as well go along with Alistair Rannoch's demand because she was going to have to leave Sandy sooner or later anyway."

Mélanie took a drink of stout. It tasted more bitter than usual. "I can see how she'd think that."

"You can't agree."

"No. Of course not. But I've always been worried about what lies in store for her and Sandy."

Kitty wiped a trace of moisture from the side of her tankard. "You'd think at this point we'd all be used to the idea that improbable couples can make a success of things."

"You'd think we'd all be used to the idea that in this world things are viewed in degrees. Degrees of birth. Degrees of scandal. The British aristocracy wouldn't have survived so long if they couldn't be flexible to a certain extent about whom they admit to their number. But selling yourself crosses a line."

"We've all sold ourselves."

"You know what I mean."

Kitty frowned. "Thinking back, I was trading my body for information before I quite admitted I was doing it. And I bartered myself to my first husband. Is it really any more shocking if men are leaving money on the table?'

"Only in the way it's viewed by the so-called polite world."

"Mélanie—"

"All right." Mélanie closed her arms over the silk and lace of her bodice . "I can't but look at Bet and Sandy and think that if Malcolm had known the truth about me—not my being a spy, what I was before that—he probably wouldn't have married me."

28

"I think you're doing Malcolm a disservice."

"Maybe. That's what Malcolm says. I'm very fond of Sandy. But he isn't Malcolm."

"No, that's true. But he loves her." Kitty shook her head, dislodging a strand of tawny hair. "God help me, a year and a half ago I'm not sure I'd have admitted I believed in romantic love. But I can recognize it."

"So can I." Mélanie curved her hands round her tankard. "And it's no guarantee of a happy ending."

"You know better than to talk about endings. But they might be able to muddle along as well as the rest of us." Kitty took a drink of stout. "Muddling along is quite delightful. If we can keep Bet from doing something stupid. I feel absurd saying this, but for God's sake, don't turn into a cynic, Mélanie."

"I wouldn't dream of it. How could I when my life is so improbably happy?"

Kitty clinked her tankard to Mélanie's. "Do stop focusing on the improbable."

"Are you telling me you don't?"

"Mmm. The fact that Julien and I can even use the word happy is improbable."

"Precisely."

As if on cue, their husbands came down the stairs into the common room.

Kitty held her tankard out to Julien as the men joined them at the table. "You look as you though you could do with this."

Julien took a long swallow of stout. "Robby was obviously set up. That much is clear from his story. But not who is behind it."

"I can tell you that." Kitty took the tankard as Julien handed it back to her. "Mélanie and Malcolm would say it's a version of *Measure for Measure*. Only the Angelo isn't asking the Isabella to go to bed with him. Or anyone. Rather the reverse."

"Who?" Malcolm asked.

"Alistair Rannoch." Kitty looked from Malcolm to her husband.

"He told Bet he has the power to get Robby acquitted. If she leaves Sandy."

"Christ." Malcolm dropped into a chair beside Mélanie and reached for her tankard. "Now I need this. And why the hell didn't I see this coming?"

"Alistair Rannoch had a lot of moves open to him," Kitty said. "I was just telling Mélanie you couldn't have predicted he'd make this one."

"Still." Malcolm turned the tankard on the table top. "I knew I needed to warn Sandy that Alistair was alive. I just didn't get to it soon enough."

"We only just learnt about Alistair," Mélanie said.

"An eternity in the midst of a mission."

"This is life," Kitty said.

"Our life is a mission." Malcolm shot a look at Julien.

"Of course, I didn't know." Julien had moved to a chair beside Kitty. "Though you're right that we probably should have seen it coming even if we couldn't have guessed Alistair would move so soon. Given we know Alistair is focused on Sandy. If I'd kept a proper eye on Robby—"

"Darling." Kitty took her husband's hand. "That won't help."

"Quite right." Julien squeezed her fingers. "I need to see Uncle Hubert. Alistair's not the only one who can bring influence to bear."

"And I should see the duke," Malcolm said. "Or Fitzroy."

"I can talk to Harriet Somerset," Mélanie said. "We have the Waterloo connection."

"Apparently Harriet and young Charlotte are at Apsley House," Malcolm said. "We can have a look at where the shot may have come from as well."

"I'll wait here for Bet." Kitty took a drink of stout. "I'm very much afraid she may try to do something foolish."

CHAPTER 5

*R*aoul O'Roarke opened the door of the Rannoch house in Berkeley Square to be greeted by his granddaughter, who hurtled into his knees.

"Someone shot the duke," Jessica announced.

"Which duke?" Raoul O'Roarke asked, scooping up Jessica.

"Wellington." Colin followed his sister into the hall, along with Amy and Jamie Craven, with Simon Tanner bringing up the rear.

"Is he hurt?" Emily, Raoul's stepdaughter, ran out of the library to join them.

"He's all right." Simon pushed the front door to as they all moved into the hall. "The bullet struck someone else. It looks as though the man who was wounded is going to be all right. But there've been complications."

"Robby's been arrested," Colin said.

"Newgate," Jamie added.

"Bow Street," Jessica said.

"Mélanie and Malcolm are saving him," Amy said.

Laura, Raoul's wife, appeared behind Emily, toddler Clara clinging to her skirts. "It sounds as though you're in the midst of an adventure." She stroked Clara's hair as Clara looked up at her with anxious eyes.

Simon looked from Laura to Raoul. "I don't know a great deal. Mélanie's gone to Bow Street with Nan Lucan."

Colin looked at Raoul. "You should go help them."

"A bit more information would help first," Laura said. "Come into the library."

They moved into the library with the children offering three or four different versions of what had happened. But before Raoul had even poured whisky for the adults and Laura had offered the children lemonade, another rap sounded at the door. Raoul went into the hall again, this time to find Sam Lucan on the doorstep. "Thank God you're home," Sam said. "Robby's—"

"Been arrested." Raoul pulled Sam into the hall and closed the door behind him. "We're getting the story from Simon, but I hope you have more details."

"He didn't do it," Sam said. "I don't think he did it. And we have to save him, regardless."

"Of course," Raoul said. "Let's get to work."

∾

JULIEN SLAPPED his gloves down on his uncle's desk. "Robby Simcox is in custody."

Hubert Mallinson looked up at him over the top of his spectacles. "I didn't put him there."

"For once I believe you." Julien pushed aside a stack of papers and perched on the edge of the desk, much as he would have done when his uncle was Lord Carfax and Julien was his agent, presumed dead and living in the shadows with a charge of treason hanging over him. Save that now it was Julien who was Lord Carfax and in possession of the desk in Carfax House from which Hubert had once presided over a vast intelligence network. Hubert might have a smaller house and a different desk, but he was still Britain's unofficial spymaster. "Alistair Rannoch is using Robby to pressure Bet Simcox."

Hubert frowned. "Sandy Trenor's mistress?"

"You've met her."

"Once or twice. Amelia was rather shocked."

"Lucinda seems to get on well with her." Lucinda was Hubert's youngest daughter. Remarkably sensible, in Julien's opinion.

"Yes, that's part of what bothered Amelia." Hubert leaned back in his chair and pushed his spectacles up on his nose. "Alistair's trying to pressure Miss Simcox into leaving Trenor?"

"That seems to be what he wants. And before you say you don't care—"

"Anything Alistair wants is problematic. What did Robby Simcox do?"

"Supposedly shot a pistol at the Duke of Wellington's carriage. And struck a bystander."

"Supposedly?"

"He says he didn't. And I'm inclined to think he's too intelligent. And too responsible."

Hubert's brows drew together. "Didn't you hire him in St. Giles?"

"And he took his job seriously. Protecting a man you were trying to have killed."

Hubert returned Julien's gaze, his own cool and steady. "Your point being?"

"Robby's morals are considerably better than yours or mine. I want him out."

Hubert shifted his silver pen on the tooled leather ink blotter. "The Rannochs are the ones who can prove him innocent."

"They're working on that. But proving him innocent may not be enough. Alistair has someone pressuring Sidmouth."

Hubert's frown deepened. "Who?"

"I don't know. But I'm sure you can find out. And apply counterpressure." Julien slammed his hand down on a stack of papers covered in code and leaned towards his uncle. "Simcox is one of mine. He's in this because he went to work for me."

"He's in this because his sister is sleeping with Trenor."

"She moved in with Trenor because of the danger to Robby. Thanks to you."

Hubert again refused to take the bait. Which wasn't surprising. In his mind, attempting to have Gerald Lumley killed had been a perfectly pragmatic decision. "No sense in fighting old battles, Julien."

"I'm not. I'm asking you to help now. You got Simon out of Newgate."

"And used up considerable leverage with Sidmouth doing so."

Julien moved the stack of papers onto the ink blotter, letting his gaze linger on the code. "Don't tell me you don't have enough leverage to manipulate Sidmouth indefinitely."

"I'm no longer Lord Carfax."

"And don't hold that over me."

"I'm not," Hubert said. "It's a statement of fact. Some of the power I used to wield by virtue of being Lord Carfax is now yours."

"You still have plenty of other power. I'm asking you to use some of that to find out who's behind the pressure to arrest Robby Simcox, and to get him released."

Hubert raised a brow. "Is that a threat?"

"My dear uncle. We each know we could ruin the other. That's the basis of our current truce. No, I'm not threatening you. You owe me for taking this bloody title and all that goes with it and attempting to do something with it in a world I cheerfully wished at the devil. I've become something far closer to an English gentleman than I ever wanted to be. The least you can do is oblige me in this."

≈

"I'D BE SURPRISED if it was just a random gunshot." Raoul studied a sketch he and Sam had done of the area where the shooting had taken place, based on Sam's intelligence. They were at one end of the library, while Laura and Simon and the children were at the other. "We haven't heard of other shootings at demonstrations. There weren't even rocks thrown at this one. It sounds like something planned, not random, done by a professional."

"It didn't kill the duke," Sam said.

"Maybe it wasn't meant to. Maybe it was just meant to create havoc. Not that many people own pistols."

"True enough," Sam said. "To think I used to make a good living dealing guns." He had had a very successful enterprise supplying weapons during the Peninsular War. Mostly to the French, like Raoul, but to the British and the guerrilleros at times as well. "Yes, I know." Sam put up a hand. "Much better not have so many guns about. I'm a father and respectable citizen now. More or less respectable. London's got enough problems without people going about shooting."

Raoul reached out to pet Berowne, the cat, who had jumped up on the table. "Have you heard any rumors of anyone's hiring for a job like this?"

Sam scratched his head. "No. But as I said, I'm almost completely respectable these days. I don't need to hire anyone for that sort of work, and those that are hiring don't talk to me. I went for a pint at the Green Dragon last week and the taproom went quiet as a churchyard when I walked in. Like I was an informant. You're the one who's still trying to bring governments down."

"I'm not trying to—"

"You are in Spain."

"The Liberals are now the government in Spain," Raoul said. "If a contested government."

"You might still be hiring people to do undercover work." Sam sat back in his chair and fixed Raoul with a hard gaze. "Don't tell me you aren't."

"I'd be a fool to waste breath trying to. Time is one thing we don't have now." Raoul scratched Berowne under the chin and retrieved the sketch before it could become a cat bed. "Where would someone go to engage an agent for a job like this?"

"Depends on who it is doing the hiring."

"But you said they got quiet at the Green Dragon when you walked in?"

"Well, yes." Sam frowned. "Didn't think much of it. No denying I'm not one of the lads anymore. But thinking back—it was a bit more extreme than usual."

Raoul pushed himself to his feet. "Let's start there."

CHAPTER 6

*a*psley House gleamed pale and imposing in the lamplight on the edge of the dark mass of Hyde Park. Shouts carried on the breeze as Malcolm and Mélanie approached down Piccadilly. They had elected to walk for speed and because carriages seemed to draw unwelcome attention at the moment. Malcolm paused and felt Mélanie tighten her fingers on his arm. A crowd were still milling in front of Apsley House's columned portico. Smaller than what Robby had described, but substantial nevertheless. Malcolm jerked his head and led the way to a side entrance.

"Where you go for secret meetings with the duke?" Mélanie looked up at him. In two minutes at the Brown Bear without a looking glass, she had pinned her walnut-brown hair up more formally than she'd had it earlier in the evening and coaxed ringlets to fall about her face. The peridot earrings and necklace he'd given her last Christmas caught the lamplight and the green embroidery on her lace gown shimmered. She might have been on her way to one of Wellington's Waterloo banquets rather than on a mission to save a man's life.

"Mmm. Let's say unofficial meetings." Meetings he hadn't told his wife about. They might now be allies with most secrets in the open, but she was still a former Bonapartist agent who had worked very industriously against Wellington and the British forces.

Malcolm rapped at the door three times, paused, rapped twice more. A short time later a footman admitted them to a narrow entryway, very different from the imposing main entrance hall they entered for Wellington's annual Waterloo banquet, with marble and gilt and a naked statue of Napoleon Bonaparte at the base of the stairs. The private quarters at Apsley House and the public rooms were as different as an informal piano recital and a grand opera.

The footman conducted them to a sitting room with white-painted walls and comfortable furniture. Fitzroy and Harriet Somerset were sitting together on a tapestry settee by the unlit fireplace, but both got to their feet.

"It was good of you to come," Fitzroy said when the footman had withdrawn. "I should have realized you'd have heard by now, with your sources."

"We don't want to intrude," Malcolm said. "But we were concerned." Leaving aside for the moment that they were investigating.

Fitzroy nodded, though his gaze said he perhaps saw more. "The duke's with Castlereagh and Sidmouth. But we're glad of the company."

"You're all right?" Mélanie went to Harriet and squeezed her hands.

"Only shaken," Harriet said. Her brown eyes were steady, but remembered fear roiled their depths, and her glossy dark curls looked as though they had been haphazardly pinned back into place after she ran her fingers through them. "I was about to go up and check on Charlotte. I got her to sleep, but I'm afraid she'll wake and be frightened. Do you want to come with me?"

"Of course. It must have been so terrifying for both of you.

Though Colin and Jessica always seem much more unflappable in the face of danger than I fear they will be."

Fitzroy watched their wives leave the room. Then he turned back to Malcolm, his gaze hardening slightly. The weight of their friendship hung between them. Nights by campfires and in leaky bivouacs in the Peninsula. The muddy field at Waterloo, where Malcolm had helped get a wounded Fitzroy to safety. And political debates in recent years, where they'd found themselves on opposite sides.

"You aren't here just to offer sympathies, are you?" Fitzroy said.

"Not solely," Malcolm said. "But you can't think we aren't concerned."

"You're a good friend, Malcolm." Fitzroy's mouth tightened. "I don't doubt you're concerned for your friends. But I also suspect you think this attack was justified."

"Fitzroy, for God's sake. When have you known me to condone violence against civilians? Or anyone, if we can help it."

"You might mention that to your friends."

"Who? Who among my friends do you think would shoot a pistol at anyone?"

"The one who's been arrested, to begin with. I understand he works for Julien Carfax. Which I assume is why you're here."

Malcolm folded his arms across his chest. "Robby Simcox is wrongly accused."

"Are you saying you wouldn't defend him if he'd done it? Your friend Roger Smythe has defended protesters in court who've done worse."

"I think everyone has the right to protest. I think people driven beyond endurance will do unconscionable things. There's a difference between understanding and condoning. But Simcox is innocent."

"You'd say that anyway."

"Not really. I wouldn't think it would work."

"Christ, Malcolm." Fitzroy stared at him. "Harriet was in that carriage. And Charlotte. And a man who just happened to be in the crowd is seriously injured."

"Which is why it's vital to learn who really did this. Simcox was set up. He has enemies."

"Because he works for Julien Carfax?"

"And his sister—"

"Is young Trenor's mistress. Are you saying Trenor's family are behind this?"

"It's not clear who is behind this. But Miss Simcox is being pressured over her brother. I don't think you want to separate two sincerely attached young people."

"She's a—"

"Don't, Fitzroy."

"Malcolm, I know your sensitivity and I commend your chivalry towards women of all sorts—"

"Don't let Mélanie hear you talk that way. And I wouldn't call appreciation of humanity chivalry."

"—but this relationship Trenor has with Miss Simcox can't continue indefinitely, in any case."

"I don't see why that should necessarily be true."

Fitzroy's gaze clashed with Malcolm's, as their fencing foils had in the past. "I know your theories about all men—"

"People—"

"—being equal. But this isn't theory. It's practical reality. Trenor is Marchmain's son. Almost the heir, since his brother's disgrace. He can't go on like this."

"We could have a lengthy debate on that. But regardless, however much we may disagree, you don't want to see an innocent man go to prison. Or the gallows."

Fitzroy glanced away. His jaw tightened. "What are you asking of me?"

"Help me learn the truth."

"I don't know the truth."

"You know more than I do. Go back to the beginning with me."

Fitzroy released his breath and gave a curt nod. He went to a table with decanters, poured two glasses of port, and gave one to Malcolm. "Ask."

"How did it start?"

Fitzroy moved to a bottle green velvet armchair and waved Malcolm to the one opposite. "We thought we could have a quiet outing. Before the trial resumes. A treat for Charlotte. Time with Uncle Arthur. We went down to Richmond for the afternoon. It hardly seemed likely to draw protest."

"These days everything is drawing protest." Malcolm took a drink of port.

"Yes, well, Richmond was fine. I noticed a few protesters in the streets as we got back to London. It was worse closer to Apsley House. I didn't think much of it at first. It's annoying, but we've got used to it. But Charlotte didn't like it. Damn it—"

"Yes, I know," Malcolm said.

"And Harriet didn't like it. Which set me on edge." Fitzroy downed half his port, though he was the sort to sip. "Then we could feel the carriage jostled, and it was clear the coachman was having trouble maneuvering. I looked at Wellington and I could tell he was about to get out and remonstrate, but I feared that would be worse. He may have saved Britain five years ago, but the multitude have short memories."

At another time, Malcolm might have debated the wisdom of Wellington's positions on the Corn Laws and a host of other initiatives with Fitzroy, as he had in the past. Instead he took a drink of port and sat forwards in his chair. "And then?"

"I started to reach across the carriage and stop the duke from getting up, when we heard the gunshot. You can imagine my terror. Then I realized none of us had been struck. And it broke the crowd. We were able to get to the door and hurry inside."

"Did you see where the shot came from?"

"No." Fitzroy turned his glass in his hand. "I didn't see anything at all."

41

KITTY HURRIED down the stairs of Carfax House to find Julien in the hall, sweeping his hat from his head. He looked up and met her gaze as she stopped midway down the stairs.

"Children asleep?"

"Just. They weren't when I got home. They know something's up."

"I'd be disappointed in them if they didn't." Julien set his hat on the Boulle cabinet where they kept the basket for calling cards.

Kitty ran down the remainder of the steps. So much had happened since she'd kissed him goodbye when he left for Brooks's. They'd been tangled in the same mission with no time to talk except those few minutes at the Brown Bear with Malcolm and Mélanie. "Quite a night."

He touched her cheek. "Quite."

"Hubert—"

"Says he'll help. I may believe him. He also claims not to have enough influence. Which I don't believe at all."

"He's careful about where he'll use his influence." Kitty considered the man who had once been her spymaster as well.

"Always. He says he's not sure whom Alistair is using."

Kitty took her husband's hand and pulled him into the library. All the rooms at Carfax House were too big to be comfortable, but the hall with its soaring ceiling and marble-tiled floor felt particularly remote. "You don't know anything more that might be useful?"

Julien stopped two steps into the library. "Kitkat, at this point don't you think I'm sharing what I know about Alistair?"

Kitty looked up at him in the lamplight. "Probably."

Julien raised a brow. "Probably?"

"Julien, don't you think it's a given none us believes the others are sharing everything about anything?"

"Fair enough." He took her other hand and pulled her to a

velvet armchair big enough to hold both of them. "I didn't have any whiff this was in the works. I didn't have any whiff anything was in the works. I suspect Gelly didn't either, though I can't be sure."

Malcolm's sister Gisèle was undercover as an ally of Alistair's. Julien, who had been working with her since she was teenager, knew more about what she was doing than any of them, but even he didn't know all of it.

Kitty let Julien pull her into the chair beside him. "I'm afraid Bet will leave Sandy before we can resolve this."

Julien slid a steadying arm behind her back. "Trenor has too much mettle to let her do that."

"A man can't stop a woman from leaving."

"No, but in this case he could go after her."

"Alistair knows that. He told her she had to leave Sandy for another man. To make it believable."

Julien frowned. "Trenor wouldn't believe any masquerade she could pull off."

"Sandy's young. Jealousy can play tricks on one. We're more than a decade older and it's played tricks on us."

Julien leaned back in the chair and drew her against him. "Yes, well, if you tried to convince me you were leaving me when your brother—or cousin, in your case—was in danger, I'd put the pieces together. Though I would wonder if you'd finally seen through me."

"Precisely."

Julien's face went serious. "We won't let them make a mull of it."

"You can't always fix things for everyone, Julien."

"We can try." Julien gave a wry smile. "Not that I ever used to do so. I was more inclined to be bemused by how much people round me seemed to waste their energies on emotions I could do very well without. In theory. Now I want them to—"

Kitty watched her husband's expression as he broke off, seemingly bemused by his own words. "Julien, you aren't really going to say 'be as happy as we are'?"

"You know I've always dared to say anything. Even at risk of shocking my wife."

"Damn it, I've been thinking the same thing." Kitty looked down at the sleeve of her gown. The lines in the corded silk blurred before her eyes. "I've turned into a romantic."

Julien reached out and touched her cheek. "My love, who but a romantic could have taken the impossible risk of marrying me? Unless you want to call that madness. But then, Shakespeare equated lunatics and lovers."

"Oh, well. All the most interesting people are a bit mad. And it may take a bit of madness to see the world clearly."

"I hope Trenor and Bet are mad enough to see that it would be true insanity to walk away from each other for the sake of a world they should be laughing at."

Kitty leaned back in the chair, her hands linked behind his neck. "It's easier to laugh at a world from inside it, Julien."

"Trenor's as much an insider as I am. Or Alistair Rannoch wouldn't be so focused on him."

"Bet isn't. And a fortune can cushion one against a great deal."

"None of us would let them starve. You know that."

"I'm not sure *they* know it. And Bet doesn't want to separate Sandy from his family. At least I didn't have to worry about that with you."

"Ha. If only you had separated me from Uncle Hubert."

Kitty settled her hands on his shoulders. "Confess it, Julien. Half the allure of marrying me was that you thought your uncle was so against it."

"Oh sweetheart. You can't possibly think that."

"So if he'd encouraged you to propose, you'd have done it without a second thought?"

"Well—I confess that whenever Uncle Hubert encourages me to do anything, I'm deeply suspicious and have to ponder what I should beware of. And part of the reason I was in such a hurry to get married was that I was afraid he'd try to interfere. But you can't think—" He studied her face, as though looking for clues beneath their banter. "I wanted to be with you. I was willing to do it on any terms, but I wanted a formal commitment. I'd have wanted to get married sooner or later, no matter what. I hope you know that."

"At the risk of a cliché—yes." Kitty pulled his head to her own and kissed him. "But it is nice to hear you say it."

Julien slid his fingers into her hair and lingered for several delicious moments, then reluctantly disengaged himself and pushed himself to his feet. "I should go back to see Robby."

"I've been thinking I should check on Bet. She said Sandy was out for the evening, and she wouldn't do anything before he got back, but I hate to think of her being alone."

Julien bent down and kissed her again. "We'll both be home at the same time at some point before dawn. Or we'll end up in Berkeley Square or back at the Brown Bear."

Kitty saw Julien out the front door, then started back upstairs to look in on the children and fetch her cloak. Perhaps it was just that she couldn't bear to be idle with so much going on, but she didn't like the idea of Bet's being alone. But she had barely reached the half landing when she heard the doorbell. It was long past when they released the footmen from duty, so she ran down the stairs, half expecting the Rannochs, to find Nan Lucan on the doorstep.

"It's Bet," Nan said without preamble. "I went round to the Albany because I didn't like her being alone."

"Nor do I. I was just going to call on her myself."

"She's not there." Nan pushed her tangled curls back from her face with an impatient hand. "I'm afraid she's gone and left Sandy. And she's going to do it as Mr. Rannoch said and leave no doubt of her intentions."

CHAPTER 7

*S*andy Trenor set down his opera glasses. There wasn't much point in looking round in any case. Bet was at home, because this was one of his duty evenings out with his parents. He'd kissed her goodbye and told her he'd try not to be late, and she'd given him one of those smiles that still made his heart turn over, and told him not to worry. After he and his parents settled in the box, he'd waved to Harry and Cordelia Davenport, who were across the theatre, and to his friends Allston and Lavering and to a few others. But he didn't have any interest in who was with whom. Not that he'd ever cared much about that, but it seemed even sillier now.

"Lady Cecily Manners just came in," his mother said, glasses trained down the line of boxes. "With her grandmother, the dowager marchioness. We must see them at the interval. Don't you think she has grown up lovely?"

Cecily Manners was a blur of blonde ringlets and a frothy white dress. Sandy remembered her with scraped knees in Hyde Park about ten years go. And he had a vivid memory of stepping on her toes at a children's ball. She'd been a few inches taller than he was then. "Lovely," he said in a dutiful voice. And then he cursed himself. Why did he keep up this pretense with his mother that he had any interest in any of the girls she tried to draw to his notice?

He cast a sidelong glance at his father. The man he still thought of as his father. The man who still seemed to think of him as his son. Lord Marchmain was studying the evening's programme. As though aware of Sandy's regard, he looked up with a faint, almost abashed expression. Not for the first time, Sandy wondered what his father really thought. About any number of things. "Always good to renew acquaintances," Marchmain said.

"Of course it is." Lady Marchmain surveyed the theatre again. "Why else does one go to the opera?"

"Well, there is the music, my dear."

Lady Marchmain shifted to look in the other direction, her sapphire necklace sparkling in the light from the sconces. "Oh, don't be difficult, Marcus."

A stir across the theatre caught Sandy's eye. A fair-haired woman in red slipping into Allston and Lavering's box. Bending over to speak with Allston quite familiarly. Odd, he hadn't heard Allston had a new mistress. She looked—Sandy started, half jumped out of his chair, gripped the arms, and sat back. Good God. It was Bet.

The first chords of music sounded, but after the overture, Sandy made an excuse about fetching more champagne and made his way along the passage to Allston's box. He walked through the antechamber and into the box without hesitation. He and his friends never stood on ceremony. Lavering was sitting at the end of the box nearest the stage, beside a girl with nut brown ringlets whom he'd been seeing for a while. A former opera dancer named Sallie. Or maybe Susie. Allston and Bet were near the rail at the nearer end, chairs close together. Bet spun round in her chair and jerked with surprise.

"Allston." Sandy clapped his friend on the shoulder while on stage Figaro and Susanna sang about their wedding. "Thank you for looking after Bet. It's damnable she couldn't come to the theatre with me."

Allston, who had flushed, gave a rough laugh. "Sorry, old chap. But all's fair in love and war, don't you know?"

"Sandy." Bet sprang to her feet and put out a gloved hand. "Don't—"

"Don't what?" Sandy caught her hand and squeezed it. "Did you think I'd mind—"

The color drained from Bet's skin, leaving bright spots of rouge on her cheekbones. "Well, I thought—"

"Civilized of you," Allston said. "Most fellows would cause a dustup."

"Why should I mind?" Sandy folded Bet's hand between both his own. "I'm delighted Bet got out for the evening. Good of you to keep an eye on her."

Lavering gave a rough laugh. "Is that what they're calling it now?"

"Why can't you talk like he does?" Sallie—or Susie—asked.

"Sandy—" Bet disengaged her fingers from Sandy's clasp and curled her hand round Allston's arm with a sort of determination. "I came here to be with Mr. Allston."

"Well, yes. I can see you wouldn't want to come to the theatre alone. I know how much you like the opera. Should have thought of setting up a party for you when I had to go off."

"Christ, Trenor," Lavering said. "Don't you know when someone's served you a turn?"

"I left, Sandy," Bet said, as though the words were jerked from her. "I left to see Mr. Allston. I left—you. I'm not going back."

Sandy stared at her. Her words seemed to spin in the air, like pieces of a puzzle he couldn't put together. Chords clashed from the orchestra pit though he couldn't make sense of the melody. "You—"

"It was time." Her voice was strained like a coat about to break at the seams. "Past time."

"Past time for what?"

"Past time we realized this had to end."

"Can't you take a hint, Trenor?" Allston demanded. "She decided she prefers me. No sense making a fuss about it. What can I do when she so obligingly accepted my invitation?"

"Don't fuss, Trenor," Lavering said. "Not worth spoiling a friendship over a common—"

Sandy's fist smashed into Lavering's face before he could finish. Lavering tumbled backwards, upending two gilded chairs, a champagne cooler, and three glasses. Champagne spurted in the air. Wood snapped and crystal shattered. Sallie-or-Susie screamed. Bet grabbed Sandy.

Lavering pushed himself to his feet and seized the lapels of Sandy's coat. Bet stumbled and fell to the ground. Sandy turned to catch her. Lavering aimed a blow at Sandy's shoulder, knocking him to the champagne-soaked floor. Sandy pushed himself to his feet and grabbed Lavering by the throat. Someone gripped him from behind. Not Bet this time. Someone taller.

"Let's get out of here," Harry Davenport said. "We have a much finer vintage of champagne in our box."

Sandy jerked instinctively against the grip on his arms.

"Not now." Davenport's voice was quiet, steady, and lethal in his ear. "Not here. Bet deserves better."

Sandy drew a breath and glanced round for Bet to see that Cordelia Davenport had an arm round her. "I'm so glad to see you here," Cordelia said. "I was quite despairing of running into a friend tonight."

"Lady Cordelia—" Bet started to pull away.

"You can't fail us. Oh, is this your reticule? We mustn't leave it." Cordelia scooped up the embroidered reticule from the wreckage of splintered wood and smashed crystal and cast a dazzling smile at Allston, Lavering, and Sallie-or-Susie. "Do pray excuse us. It seems an age since we've had a chance to talk with Bet and Sandy."

It had in fact been two nights ago at the Carfaxes', but the words seemed to work on Lavering, Allston, and Sallie-or-Susie. Lavering and Allston scrambled out of the way and sketched bows as Cordelia shepherded Bet out of the box. Harry gripped Sandy's arm and propelled him after. Over the blood pounding in his head, Sandy was vaguely aware of a blur of gazes turned in their direction while Figaro cursed Count Almaviva's betrayal.

They went down the passage, past a crossfire of more interested gazes, and into the antechamber of another box. Bet pulled away from Cordelia and turned to Sandy the moment they were inside. "Are you all right?"

"All right?" Sandy put up a hand to his neckcloth and realized it was crumpled in a way that would shock his valet. "Of course I am. Are you? What insult did Allston offer you before I got there?"

"Sandy." Bet clutched the reticule Cordelia had retrieved, a reticule Sandy had given her for Christmas. "I didn't want to make a scene, but I meant it. I came here tonight to see Mr. Allston."

Sandy stared at her. "What did they do to you? What are they holding over you?"

"Who?"

"My parents. Or Mama, at least. That's why you're doing this, isn't it? They're forcing you to—"

"Sandy—" Bet touched his wrist, then dropped her hand back to her side. "It has to end. No one had to force me to realize that."

"No one," Harry said, "in my opinion, should remain in a relationship they do not wish to continue. But I confess I do share Sandy's concern. You didn't seem to be contemplating this change when we saw you the night before last."

Bet gripped her hands together, her fingers working over the silver clasp. She wasn't wearing her ring, Sandy realized. The aquamarine he'd given her for her birthday, that she hadn't taken off ever since, even in bed. "I've known it for a long time. I was just avoiding facing it."

"Known what?" Sandy blurted the words out, and then realized he perhaps should have thought more before he spoke.

Bet's gaze locked on his own and for the moment it was as though there were only the two of them in the room. Though not in a good way. "That we couldn't go on."

"But why now?" Harry's voice was level and practical, the voice Sandy had heard him use when he was talking through a case. "What made you decide tonight was the time to make such a monumental change? A change that—forgive me if I am wrong—I do not think you wished to make?"

Bet's sharp breath cut through the melody echoing through from the stage, like a knife ripping velvet curtains. "I knew we couldn't go on."

"Why?" Harry's gaze was kind, but his voice was inexorable. He was leaning against the gold damask-covered wall of the antechamber, legs crossed at the ankle, as though he had all the time in the world. "Why now?"

Bet glanced to the side.

"Forgive us, Bet," Cordelia said, "but we're all concerned that you've been subject to some compulsion. If someone has threatened you, or tried to coerce you—"

The door to the antechamber burst open. Kitty—Lady Carfax —ran in, a black velvet cloak swirling round her, her red-gold hair coming loose from its pins. "Thank goodness." Her gaze went straight to Bet and then to Sandy. "I was afraid—have you told him?"

"Lady Carfax—" Bet put out a hand. "No. Please."

"Please what?" Sandy said.

Kitty looked from Cordelia to Harry. "Do you know?"

"No," Cordelia said. "But we'd very much like to find out. That is, not because we want to pry, but for Bet's sake. So we can help, if possible."

51

"Someone's threatening Bet to make her leave me," Sandy said. He dug his fingers into his hair. "That is, I think so. Unless I'm being a fool. Unless I'm a terrible judge of character. Which is entirely possible. In which case, perhaps she really is just tired of me." He looked into Bet's eyes and saw anguish and felt a rush of relief. Guilt promptly washed over him.

"Lady Carfax—" Bet said in a voice like broken glass.

"Damnation." Kitty leaned against the door of the antechamber. "I hate people who interfere. I believe in everyone's right to make choices for themselves. I particularly believe in a woman's right to do so. But I can't stand by while you throw your life away."

"I'm not—"

"And Sandy's." Kitty's gaze shot to Sandy. "Sandy has a right to decide this for himself. What happens to your relationship is up to the two of you, but don't throw it away for this. Among other things, there's no guarantee it will work."

"My parents," Sandy said.

"No," Bet said. "Yes. Sandy—"

"He has to know," Kitty said. "He deserves that. For his own protection."

Bet drew a shuddering breath. Her nails dug into the embroidery on her reticule. Her gaze shot to Cordelia and then Harry.

"If it's what I think it is, he has to know," Cordelia said.

Harry inclined his head. Odd, for such a sharp-tongued man, he could have the kindest gaze.

Bet turned her gaze back to Sandy. "Alistair Rannoch is alive."

Sandy was so focused on Bet he hadn't been thinking of anything else. Let alone a man whom he had assumed was dead. Whose connection to him had seemed to matter more in terms of his relationship with his own parents (the people he would always think of as his parents). He was used to the unexpected in his interactions with the Rannochs, but—"He can't be. People don't just—"

"Julien did," Kitty said. "Thank goodness."

"Yes, but—" Sandy stared at her. Difficult now to remember that Julien Carfax—who was really Arthur Mallinson, though he wouldn't let anyone call him that—had been presumed dead since before Sandy was born. "Good God. But why—"

"We don't know," Harry said. "Not yet. But Alistair Rannoch appears to be trying to clear his name."

Sandy turned to the Davenports. "You know too?"

"Only very recently," Harry said.

"And Malcolm and Mélanie—"

"We all only just found out," Cordelia said. "Malcolm was planning to tell you. It all rather got away from us."

"Yes, I can see that." Sandy dug a hand into his hair again. "But—" He swung his gaze to Bet. "Alistair threatened you?"

"No, he—" Bet swallowed, looked at Kitty, looked back at Sandy. "Robby's in trouble. Mr. Rannoch offered to help him."

"If you left me."

"Yes."

"Oh God, Bet." Sandy crossed to her in two steps and gripped her hands. "Why didn't you tell me?"

"Why do you think?" Bet jerked her hands away. "I have to protect Robby, Sandy. You must see that."

"Of course we have to protect him." Sandy took a step back and smoothed the shoulders of his coat. "Where's Alistair Rannoch? I need to see him."

"Sandy, no." Bet took a step forwards. "This isn't your fight."

"Whose fight is it, then? Don't mean to be arrogant, but you can't tell me he'd be trying to coerce you if it weren't for me."

"Malcolm and Mélanie are working on this," Kitty said. "And Julien and the rest of us."

"But Alistair isn't Malcolm's father," Sandy said. "And apparently he's mine. And he threatened Bet. If anyone's going to deal with this, it should be me." He glanced at Cordelia and then at Harry.

53

Harry inclined his head. "You have a point. But let me come with you."

Sandy met Harry's gaze, conscious of relief and abashed that he felt it. But then, he'd never seen himself as the sort to claim to be able to handle everything. He had no illusions about being a hero. But it was past time he took responsibility for his life and the people he cared about. "Thank you." He swung his gaze to Bet. "Where can we find Alistair Rannoch? He must have given you some way to contact him."

Bet swallowed.

"You're very brave, Bet," Kitty said. "Braver than I am, I think. But don't make the mistake of trusting Alistair Rannoch to save your brother. If it comes down to trusting him or trusting the Rannochs and the Davenports and Julien and me and Sandy, what does your instinct tell you?"

Bet released her breath. "He's at the Green Dragon in St. Giles. In a private room upstairs. He told me he'd be there this evening."

"Thank you." Sandy squeezed her hands again, hesitated, then leaned in and kissed her. "Wait for me. I won't fail you."

CHAPTER 8

*H*arriet Somerset looked down at her daughter, sleeping in a white-painted iron bed in a floral-papered room tucked away in Apsley House. "I can still scarcely believe it."

"I'm so sorry," Mélanie said. "I can't imagine anything more terrifying than being in danger with one's children." Which, for all the dangers she had been through, was quite true. Not that there weren't more than a few times Colin and Jessica had been in danger because of her.

Harriet smoothed a quilt over Charlotte. "I've heard the stories about rocks being thrown. I've seen the protests driving through Mayfair or in the park or in Westminster. I've heard some beastly things yelled. I was frightened when I saw the crowd round the carriage. But I trusted our grooms and coachman. When the pistol went off, at first I thought it must be thunder. I mean, in the middle of London—what is the world coming to?" She glanced round at Mélanie. "Is this what it was like during the Revolution?"

"I was a baby during the Revolution," Mélanie said. That was true as well, though her parents had been revolutionary actors, not the dispossessed aristocrats of her cover story.

"I know Malcolm's politics," Harriet said. "But surely he wouldn't condone—"

"Of course not. Neither of us would."

Harriet moved through a door to an adjoining sitting room. "The man's been arrested, thank God."

Mélanie hesitated, but they needed desperately needed information and there was little time for finesse. "Are you sure they have the right man?" she asked, as she followed Harriet.

Harriet stared at her. "Dear God, Mélanie, are you on his side?"

"I'm not on the side of whoever shot at you. Whyever they did it."

"Surely that's obvious. They did it because they hate Uncle Arthur."

"Harriet." Mélanie gripped her friend's hand. "You must know it's not unheard of for the government to plant people among protesters to incite violent acts and give the protest a bad name."

"You would think that." Harriet moved to a chintz-covered settee across the room.

"You mean I'm more inclined to think it because I don't like to believe people protesting something I agree with would do something like this?" Mélanie asked as she sat beside Harriet. "That's true. But I know people I agree with can do things I disagree with." Not to mention that she'd done a number of questionable things herself. "I also know agents provocateurs are a fact."

"You agree with people yelling at Uncle Arthur?"

"I don't think yelling's very helpful. I also don't agree with much of your uncle's politics. Neither does Malcolm. You know that."

Harriet gave an unexpected smile. "Yes, Uncle Arthur says as much. He says he could never have imagined being so fond of a fire-breathing Radical. And also that he couldn't imagine a fire-breathing Radical in fact being so measured and calm."

"Malcolm is certainly that. It doesn't lessen the intensity of his feelings."

"No." Harriet pleated a fold of the shiny copper-colored gros-de-Naples of her gown between her fingers. Mélanie had a sudden image of Harriet pleating a fold of her gown in much the same way in Brussels just before the Waterloo campaign. She'd caught Harriet's gaze then and seen her fear for her husband and felt the same fear course through her. Though Mélanie had been giving information to the opposite side and had also been worried about her ex-lover and spymaster who was fighting for the French. "We've always been friends," Harriet said. "I don't want that to change."

"No," Mélanie agreed. "If—"

"Mummy."

A small voice interrupted them. Charlotte Somerset stood in the doorway, stuffed rabbit clutched in one hand, bare feet peeping out from beneath her nightdress.

Harriet stretched out a hand. "What is it, darling?"

Charlotte took a step forwards. She'd been only a few weeks old during Waterloo. Mélanie remembered her being taken for walks round the park. Harriet had gone to Antwerp with Charlotte during the campaign to protect her.

"You're talking about what happened tonight," Charlotte said.

"Well, yes." Harriet caught Charlotte's hand and squeezed it. "But there's no need for you to worry. It's all over."

"I'm not worried." Charlotte climbed onto the settee between her mother and Mélanie. "But that man's in prison, isn't he?"

"Not yet," Mélanie said. "But he's been arrested."

"And he might go to prison."

"He might." Mélanie wasn't going to go into how hard they were going to try to prevent that.

Charlotte looked between them, brows drawn together. "I don't think that man shot the gun."

"Why not?" Harriet asked.

"That's not where the shot came from."

"Darling," Harriet said, "you can't possibly remember—"

"Did you hear where it came from, sweetheart?" Mélanie asked.

Charlotte climbed into her mother's lap. "It came from the left. From the window by Uncle Arthur. The man they arrested was on the right."

"How do you know?" Harriet asked.

"I saw. I heard everyone yelling and saw them rush over and grab him. He was on the ground. Someone shoved a pistol towards him. Then he touched it. He looked confused." She looked at Mélanie. "Does that help? I don't want the wrong person to go to prison. No one would."

"No," Harriet agreed.

"So it helps?" Charlotte persisted.

Mélanie squeezed Charlotte's hand. "It might help very much indeed."

BET TUGGED AWAY from Cordelia's arm seconds after Sandy and Harry let the box. "I should go after him. He can't just go off and confront Mr. Rannoch."

"I detest men going into action and leaving women behind," Kitty said. "But Sandy does rather have a point. He's the one Mr. Rannoch is targeting. And much as I sympathize with your worrying about him, I also sympathize with someone's not wanting to be kept out of the action. Not that Julien does that often. Well, not ever. Not unless he has other reasons for keeping a mission from me."

"I can't just let him rush into the middle of this because of me," Bet said.

"Darling, he's already in the middle of it," Cordelia said. "Sandy's right, Alistair Rannoch did this because of him."

Kitty met Cordelia's gaze across the antechamber of the box. Odd to have become such good friends with someone who was such a product of the world Kitty would never belong in. "I admit at times your Sandy makes me think of my sons, but I think he's shown himself adult enough to confront Alistair Rannoch. To get through this, he's going to have to be able to do so. It's difficult seeing the person one loves run risks, but sometimes one has to do it."

Bet hugged her arms round herself. The twisted scarlet silk sleeves of her gown slid off her shoulders, but she reminded Kitty of Cordelia's young daughters. Or even of her own toddler, Genny. "Robby's not Sandy's responsibility. He's mine."

"You're Sandy's responsibility," Cordelia said.

"I'm not—"

"Don't be foolish." Kitty moved to Bet's side and put an arm round her.

"And Alistair Rannoch is Sandy's responsibility," Cordelia said.

"How did you even know I was here?" Bet asked Kitty.

"Your sister told me. She's looking for Robby's friends who were at the protest with him. I promised her I'd stop you from doing anything foolish because you were threatened."

"It won't work." Bet dashed a hand across her eyes, though she didn't attempt to pull away from Kitty. "Don't you think I don't appreciate what Sandy's doing—what you're all doing? But the risk to Robby—That's why I had to do this—"

"I don't think Sandy is going to let you leave him," Cordelia said. "Not if you're doing it to save Robby."

"And it's far more dangerous to trust Alistair Rannoch to save Robby," Kitty said.

Bet frowned. "I can see that. But I'm not sure Mr. Rannoch can be outwitted."

"We've done it before," Cordelia said. "That is, Malcolm and Mélanie have, but we've all helped. Focus on that. And decide what you want with Sandy when your brother is safe. It's your decision to make, but it should be made freely."

Bet's mouth twisted, and for a moment she looked years older. "Are we ever really free?"

"We can try to be," Kitty said. "And when we put our minds to it, we're likely to succeed."

CHAPTER 9

Sandy shot a look at Harry as they walked through the Covent Garden piazza. "Have you seen him?"

"No." Harry's voice was level but his gaze was kind. Too kind to intrude. Odd, how kind he could be. Sandy could remember a time when he'd been half afraid of Davenport. "Malcolm's only seen him once."

Sandy nodded. "It's odd. I mean, I've known for a while that he's—that he sired me or whatever you want to call it. And it made a certain sense. Of how my father—Marchmain—has always been. Though he's always been very decent to me, all things considered. But it didn't seem real somehow. I mean, Rannoch—Alistair Rannoch—was dead, or I thought he was, so it was sort of like learning some unexpected twist about a character in a book. Only the character was me in this case. And since Alistair Rannoch was gone, it would never really mean anything. I'd never known him, and I never would. Now—I don't know what to expect."

"Nor do I," Harry said.

Sandy nodded, grateful Harry didn't try to offer reassurance. "I remember Rannoch once at a party at my parents' house. In the card room. He asked if I wanted to play. I said I hadn't much taste for cards. He looked a bit disappointed. Which makes more sense now." Sandy paused, staring at a bunch of wilted violets, caught by a patch of lamplight on the blue-black paving. "I suppose I must have seen him other times. At parties, in the park, at the races. Across a theatre." He grimaced, thinking of tonight. "But I can't say I noticed much."

"No reason for you to have done so."

"Yes, but I mean—" Sandy wrenched his gaze from the wilted flowers to look at Harry. "You'd think I'd have picked up on some of it."

"What is there to pick up on? It's an accident of biology, as you said."

"It seems to mean something to Alistair Rannoch."

"Yes, well. Some men place a lot of importance on bloodlines."

"I'm not sure I would. That is—" Sandy broke off. An image shot into his mind. Bet with a baby in her arms. A toddler riding on his own shoulders. Not bloodlines. It didn't matter if it was a boy or a girl. But—"Not bloodlines. They don't matter to me. But I'd like children."

"Oh, well." Harry grinned. "That's different."

Sandy shot a look at him. "Did you always—"

"Know I wanted children? Not particularly," Harry said, as they moved into the shadows of the colonnade. "It never even occurred to me I'd get married until I met Cordy. Then—well, it was rather a tangle. I didn't think about parenthood at all until I met Livia years later. Now—it's hard to think about my life any other way. Funny—if I hadn't been lucky and met Cordy, and then if I hadn't been luckier and we'd managed to salvage our marriage, I'd have missed out on all of that."

Sandy nodded. The future, which he tended to firmly resist looking at, suddenly seemed at once more tantalizing and more frightening. "But that's not what Alistair Rannoch wants from me."

"To be honest," Harry said, "I'm not in the least sure what Alistair wants from you. That's one reason I was nervous about your talking to him."

"I have to." Sandy stopped again and looked up at Harry in the lamplight that spilled between two columns. "I can't just stand by and let him do this."

"No," Harry agreed. "I understand."

"But you don't think I'm equal to it. That's why you wanted to come with me."

Harry put a hand on his shoulder. "My dear chap. I'm quite sure you're equal to more than you realize. I'm here to support you. And I'll do my best not to let you down."

SANDY STRODE up the stairs at the Green Dragon and flung open the door without hesitation. "We need to talk. Father."

The man Sandy could scarcely remember stared across the room at him. His fingers froze round the brandy glass he held. His piercing eyes widened with surprise. Which Sandy doubted was usual for him. "Alexander. I confess I didn't expect you."

Sandy slammed the door shut behind him and Harry, who had followed him into the room. "You can't have a very high opinion of me if you thought you could threaten the woman I love and I'd simply stand by and let it happen."

Alistair Rannoch's gaze shot from Sandy to Harry. "I take it I have you to thank for this, Davenport?"

"You overrate me and underrate Trenor," Harry said. He remained by the door, a little to one side, but Sandy felt the support of his presence.

Alistair reached for the bottle on the table beside his chair. "May I pour you both a brandy?"

"No, thank you."

"Ditto." Harry was leaning against the wall, arms folded, legs crossed.

"Suit yourselves." Alistair took a drink from his own glass and set it down with care. His gaze shot to Sandy. "How long have you known?"

"That you're my father, at least in some sense of the word? I learnt last year. That you're alive? I learnt tonight."

"I imagine it was a surprise."

"Of course it was." Sandy strode forwards but paused partway across the room. He had no desire to sit down and dignify this as a civil conversation. "And of course I can't but be pleased that someone I thought dead is in fact alive. But given the lack of a relationship we've had my entire life, it can hardly be held to make much of a difference to me."

"And yet you're here."

"Because you threatened Bet."

"I don't recall doing anything of the sort." Alistair twitched a shirt cuff smooth beneath the sleeve of his coat. "I offered to attempt to assist her unfortunate brother."

"If she left me."

"Alexander." Alistair's gaze shot over Sandy's face, and for a moment there was something almost soft in those hard eyes. Something that made all Sandy's defenses spring into place, the way the fur rose on the Rannochs' cat's back when he was on his guard. "I fully admit I have not been to you what a father should be. But can you think so ill of me you imagine I take no interest in your well-being?"

"If you take an interest in my well-being, you should realize Bet is essential to my happiness."

"Essential." Alistair's mouth twisted in a dry smile that was disconcertingly kind. "It can mean so many things. And if you'll permit me to say so, as one who has lived more than twice as long as you, what seems essential to you now will almost inevitably not seem so in ten years. Even five."

"Why on earth should I take your advice about anything? You don't know me."

"I've had reports on you since you were born."

"I don't much care for that."

"Whatever you think of me, Alexander, I hope you will accept that I have your best interests at heart."

"I accept nothing of the sort."

"Happiness can seem to lie in a woman, at your age. Trust me in this, if nothing else. It won't last."

"Is that how it was for you with Arabella Rannoch?"

Sandy blurted out the words. Only after he had spoken them, when he saw the recoil in Alistair's eyes, did he realize he'd struck blood.

"My marriage to Arabella brought me a number of things. Your relationship with Bet Simcox can't do anything of the sort."

"Which rather supports that there's something very real to his relationship with Miss Simcox," Harry said. He met Alistair's gaze for a moment. "Sorry."

"You're a parent, Davenport," Alistair said. "I presume you don't want your daughters to throw their lives away."

"I trust my daughters to make their own decisions about their lives. Including whom they choose to love."

"I suspect you'll feel differently when they're grown up." Alistair's gaze shot back to Sandy. "You have a bright future ahead of you. A future I can help you secure."

"Thank you. I may not be brilliant, but I'm not interested in having anyone help secure my future. That is—I suppose my parents have helped me. Can't deny that. I mean, I'd be a fool to say I'm not fortunate. Can't talk about that as eloquently as Malcolm, but I do realize it. I'm inestimably fortunate compared to Bet and her family. All the more reason I don't want anyone opening more doors for me. Especially you."

Alistair ran his gaze over Sandy. "You can stand up for yourself. That's good. And of course, given the company you've been keeping"—he cast a glance at Harry—"forgive me, Davenport, but there's no sense in denying reality—you have a less than flattering opinion of me. I don't ask you to change your mind all at once. I only ask you to give me a chance."

"You've chosen an odd way of going about it, by attacking Robby and attempting to come between Bet and me."

"You must forgive my concern for you. You're at an age where the decisions you make could irrevocably set the course of your life."

Sandy looked straight into the eyes of the man who had fathered him. Assuming that word even applied to it. "Like the decisions you made set you on the course you're on now?"

He saw his words strike home in Alistair's eyes. Once again he realized he'd cut more sharply than he intended. But Alistair's gaze remained steady. "I can't claim to be entirely pleased with how my life has played out. But part of making mistakes is not wanting one's son to make them as well. And I wouldn't be where I am were not for the choices I made in the past."

"And are you happy with those choices?" Sandy asked, holding Alistair's gaze.

Something jerked in the depths of Alistair's eyes. "One of the benefits of having a past to look back on is being able to advise the younger generation to make different choices. And yet, if I hadn't made those choices I wouldn't be the man I am today. I can't say I'm sorry for who I am. At my time of life, there is a certain satisfaction in still standing, still being in a position to influence the game. But I hope your life runs more smoothly than mine has done."

"My life is mine to forge."

Alistair took a drink of brandy. "But you can't deny the legacy of your birth."

"Malcolm does."

"On the contrary. Malcolm is more shaped by being Raoul O'Roarke's son than most men I could think of are shaped by their fathers."

"That's because O'Roarke raised him." Sandy had heard

66

Malcolm say that often enough. "You didn't raise me. You don't know me. But if you ever want the chance to know me, if you ever want to see me again, you'll stop pressuring Bet."

"Miss Simcox already seems aware there is no hope for your relationship."

Disquiet tugged at Sandy. He tamped it down. "That's because I haven't made my feelings plain enough. Or if it's because she doesn't want to be with me, that's between Bet and me."

"You don't have the luxury of anything's being just between the two of you, lad. I'm sure you don't want Miss Simcox made unhappy."

"If you make her unhappy," Sandy said, a memory of his brother with a knife at Bet's throat sharp in his memory, "you'll never see me again. And I'll do everything in my power to bring you down. I know that probably doesn't seem like much of a threat. But if you think I've inherited anything from you, you should be afraid of me."

Alistair Rannoch's gaze shifted over Sandy. Then he gave a slow smile. The sort of smile Sandy had seen men give when a longshot won at Ascot. "You have bottom. I wasn't sure you did."

"Is that what this was?" Sandy demanded. "A test?"

"Hardly. I was concerned about your future. I am. But I'm pleased to see your mettle."

"Don't be too pleased. I'm not like you at all. I don't like fights. I just want a quiet life."

"You haven't got a chance of that no matter what, my boy. Look at what you were born into."

"One can still escape."

"Is that what Malcolm says? He's been less adept at it than anyone."

"I wouldn't underestimate Malcolm. Or me."

"My dear Alexander. I don't underestimate you in the least."

And somehow that was the most disturbing thing of all.

67

CHAPTER 10

*R*aoul pushed his way between tables at the Green Dragon. He hadn't taken the time to don a disguise, but he was used to slipping through crowds so as to draw minimum attention. It was a way of moving with a sort of languid assurance, as though one belonged and was not going about anything out of the ordinary.

Sam jerked his head towards the corner. A red-haired man in a blue coat sat sprawled in a chair, nursing a tankard. George Dawkins. Raoul had encountered him once or twice when hiring assistance. In the old days, closer to the war, when Sam had not yet found his current employment, and Raoul had turned to him for help with unofficial missions. Not that anything Raoul did could be called official.

Dawkins's head jerked up as they approached. Wariness shot through his shoulders. "Evening, Dawkins," Sam said, planting himself in front of the table.

"What do you want, Lucan?"

"Information. Someone was hiring for a job. Started looking a week or so ago. We ran into Ned Allington on the way here. Ned said he turned the man down at the Queen's Arms and thought he was headed here."

Dawkins inched back in his chair, shoulders straight against the cracked slats. "Maybe he was."

"Don't be difficult, Dawkins. Who did he hire?"

Dawkins gave a rough laugh. "Why would I tell either of you? You've gone respectable." He jerked his gaze to Sam. "And you aren't paying this time." His gaze snapped to Raoul.

Raoul leaned across the table. Threats could be useful at times. But often an appeal to fellow feeling could be more effective than a threat. If you could convince the interrogatee they were on your side, the rest would follow, and there was far less need to worry they were coming up with lies. "I'll pay for the information. And I can promise it will go very ill for you if you don't tell." Raoul leaned closer, palms pressing into wood sticky with spilled ale and porter. "But more to the point, it will go ill for Robby Simcox. Whom I don't think you want hurt."

Dawkins's gaze widened. "Robby's a good lad. Even if he's gone respectable too."

"He's been taken up by Bow Street," Sam said. "For something he didn't do."

Dawkins reached for his tankard and took a swig. "Tom McCandless. Leastways, rumor is he got hired on by a man who was asking questions a week ago. Needed someone who could fire a pistol."

"Which this man—McCandless, if he's the one—did," Sam said. "Only he missed. And hit the wrong person."

Dawkins frowned. "McCandless wouldn't miss. He was a rifleman. I've seen him shoot the pips on an ace at forty paces. Three sheets to the wind, at that. If he hit someone, whoever's wounded is the person he meant to hit."

～

MALCOLM HELD a paper out to Roth. It bore the Duke of Wellington's seal. "Charlotte dictated her memory of what happened, and her mother wrote it down. Both her parents signed it. Wellington added his seal. Fitzroy and Harriet are prepared to bring Charlotte to talk to Sir Nathaniel, should it be necessary."

Roth studied the duke's seal. "This will hold a great deal of weight. But it's still a child's word. Even a sharp-eared child—even a sharp-eared adult—could misconstrue where a sound came from. Could misinterpret what she saw on the ground in the midst of a crisis." He looked up and met Malcolm's gaze and then Mélanie's. "I'm only saying what I suspect I will hear when I take this to Sir Nathaniel. To my mind, children have very acute instincts, and I suspect young Miss Somerset is spot on in her assessment of what happened."

"So do I." Julien looked up from the tankard of coffee he'd been nursing. He'd been at the Brown Bear when Malcolm and Mélanie got there.

Kitty, Bet, and Cordelia hurried into the room as Julien spoke. Mélanie met Cordelia's gaze for a brief instant and knew Cordelia had the whole story. No need to ask how, for now.

"Sandy's gone to see Alistair Rannoch," Bet said. "I couldn't stop him."

"Another failure on my part, not to tell him," Malcolm said.

"Harry's with him," Cordelia said.

"Sandy can handle it." Malcolm touched Bet's hand. "I may have failed, but I have great faith in him."

Bet gave a smile, warm but frayed round the edges. "Is there news about Robby?"

Roth showed her the paper Malcolm and Mélanie had brought from Apsley House.

Bet's eyes widened. "Is it enough?"

"I wish I could say yes," Roth said. "But we still have pressure being applied from we don't know where."

Julien set down his coffee and pushed himself to his feet. "I have a few more contacts I can talk to who may have heard of anything afoot."

"I'll go to Roger Smythe," Malcolm said. "In case we need to mount a defense in court. And Raoul sent word he and Sam are looking for whoever may have been the shooter."

"How do they think they can find him?" Bet asked. "Do they know people who were in the crowd?"

"They think the shooting may have been done by someone hired," Malcolm said. Raoul's brief note had confirmed something that had already been at the back of his mind.

"To shoot Wellington?" Bet asked.

"Perhaps. Or to create a disturbance."

Kitty looked at Julien. "Do I think Uncle Hubert would hire someone to shoot at Wellington to turn public opinion against the demonstrators?" Julien said. "In a minute. Though given how unpopular Wellington's been lately, I'm not sure it would work. Which doesn't mean Uncle Hubert wouldn't try it. I didn't pick up on any clue that he had when I saw him earlier tonight. But it wouldn't be the first time I'd missed cues with him."

"I can keep Robby here overnight," Roth said. "I'll make sure they don't move him while I go to Sir Nathaniel." He looked among them. "I'll let you know as soon as I know more. Meanwhile—"

"We'll do the same," Malcolm said.

RAOUL AND SAM were halfway across the taproom when they heard footsteps coming down the stairs. Raoul glanced round with instinctive wariness and found himself looking at Sandy Trenor and Harry Davenport. Sandy went still, staring at them in surprise. Harry came forwards quickly. "You've learnt something?"

"We hope so," Raoul said. "Were you in search of information?"

"In a manner of speaking. Alistair Rannoch's upstairs. Sandy wanted to talk with him. And stood up to him admirably."

"Don't know about that," Sandy said. "But I had to tell him he won't get anywhere with me by threatening Bet. I wouldn't be much of a—I wouldn't be worthy of her if I didn't do that."

"No indeed," Raoul said. "I should have guessed Alistair was behind this. And that he'd try to use Robby's plight against his sister."

"Damn it," Sam said, striding towards the stairs. "I should have a word with him myself. Or more than a word."

"Those tactics won't work on Alistair," Raoul said. "But if you don't mind, I'll have a word with him. You can update Sandy and Harry."

Alistair Rannoch pushed himself to his feet at the opening of the door. "Twice in almost as many days, O'Roarke. What have I done to deserve this?"

"You know that better than I do." Raoul pushed the door to.

"I suppose you've come to give me some sort of ultimatum."

"I understand Trenor already did that."

Alistair gave a short laugh. "He's tougher than I thought. His zeal may be misplaced, but I admire his tenacity." He reached for his brandy glass. "I imagine you're wishing me at the devil. Though I would think you'd feel a certain sympathy for a father's desire to mold his son's life in the direction he thinks is best."

Raoul moved to the chair across from Alistair. "I don't know that I ever tried to mold Malcolm. I took advantage of him. Unforgivably, one might say. But that was to win a war, not to mold him."

"I didn't mean that. I meant all the time you spent with him growing up."

"That's called parenting."

Alistair gave a short laugh. "Can you tell me you wouldn't have tried to separate him from the wrong woman?"

"I hope I wouldn't have. Assuming I could even have been sure who the 'wrong woman' was, I'm not sure I'd have succeeded if I'd tried."

"Don't talk rubbish, O'Roarke. I have no doubt you'd have succeeded."

"That's because you've always underrated Malcolm."

Alistair shot a look at him. "I've always been very aware of how much trouble Malcolm could cause in a number of ways. But he idolized you from the first."

For a moment Raoul could feel the small hand in his own, the small arms round his neck. The wonder, the terror, the longing to grasp hold of what he could, while he could. "I wouldn't call it that. But he heartily wished me at the devil a few years ago. I'm extraordinarily fortunate we're still on speaking terms."

"You've always had the devil's own luck, O'Roarke." Alistair took a drink of brandy, then poured another glass and pushed it across the table towards Raoul. "When I first met you, I didn't think you'd survive to see thirty."

Raoul met the gaze of the man who had been one of his greatest enemies and come near to destroying many of the people he loved. "I probably wouldn't have lived long past my thirtieth birthday if it weren't for you."

Alistair grunted. "I didn't have much choice about that."

"There's always a choice. Just not one we're prepared to make, at times."

"It was a hard mouthful to swallow. I wanted you dead at Dunboyne. But I have enough sense of self-preservation I didn't hesitate when Bella came to me demanding I rescue you or face ruin. Besides"—he turned his glass in his hand—"when Bella came to me so desperate to save you, I realized it wouldn't make any difference if you died. She'd feel just as strongly. In fact, your ghost might have had more of a hold on her."

Raoul picked up the glass Alistair had poured. "I doubt I ever had much of a hold on her."

"You're underrating yourself. Mind you, I still thought you'd die far before she did."

"Yes," Raoul said, "so did I." In fact, for all he'd worried about her, he'd never really imagined a life without Arabella.

Alistair took a drink of brandy, as though weighing his words with care. "I've wished you at the devil almost from the moment I met you, O'Roarke. And I still do. But I wish you'd been with Arabella in those last days."

Whatever Raoul had expected Alistair to say, it was not that. He forced down a swallow of brandy. His throat had gone rough. "I doubt it would have made a difference."

"No?" Alistair looked sideways at him. "Again, I think you're underrating yourself. Or underrating Arabella. It was hard to make sense of her. At times I'd have sworn she cared for nothing. But I have no doubt she cared for you."

"You have fewer doubts than I, then."

Alistair gave a short laugh. "You're a fool, O'Roarke." He watched Raoul for a moment. "In many ways my wife remains a mystery to me. But after she went to such lengths to get you out of Ireland, it was quite clear how she felt about you."

"Arabella never did anything for just one reason." Raoul returned Alistair's gaze. "She was a damnable person to love."

"You'd know more about that than I do."

"You're the only one who can answer that."

Alistair turned away. For a long moment, Raoul thought he wouldn't reply. "We're all capable of foolery. I'd rather Arabella was alive and with you than gone."

Without using the word love, it was a rather extraordinary statement of the emotion. "I doubt she'd be with me if she was alive."

"You wouldn't have left her. And she'd have kept coming back to you. At least on occasion."

"Perhaps." It wasn't something Raoul cared to dwell on. "Arabella and I were actually more concerned with our various causes than with each other."

"Are you telling me you could keep the two apart?"

Raoul's fingers tightened round his glass. "At times."

"Your whole relationship was built on a cause. So is Malcolm's with Mélanie. And yours with Mélanie. And yours with your current wife, I imagine."

"In different ways."

Alistair met his gaze for a long moment. "You'd do anything for them, I imagine. Just as Arabella once would have done anything for you. So I trust you'll understand why I'd do anything for Alexander."

Raoul set his glass on the table. "Aren't you afraid you're going to lose him?"

"By no means. I have no intention of losing."

CHAPTER 11

"*R*obby's being very patient," Bet said. "He wasn't the least patient as a little boy—always rushing headlong into things. But he told me to thank everyone and to say that he knew you were doing everything you could and the best thing he could do was not make things worse." She rubbed her arms, crumpling her long white gloves.

"I'm so glad." Cordelia said. "Waiting is the very devil. But things look much more hopeful than they did. There's no need—"

"For me to leave Sandy?" Bet gave a twisted smile. "On reflection, I do see that wouldn't work very well. Sandy wouldn't take it easily, and you're quite right, there's no guarantee Mr. Rannoch would do as he said he would. Probably the reverse."

"Very wise." Laura leaned forwards to refill the coffee. They were back in the Berkeley Square library. Laura and Simon had persuaded the children to go to bed, or at least got them more or less settled in the nursery. Mélanie had heard voices quiet suspiciously when she went in to check on them, and Colin had given her a sheepish grin as she bent to kiss him. Blanca and Addison, her companion and Malcolm's valet, who were an invaluable assistance in investigations, unfortunately were away visiting Addison's sister.

"But it doesn't change things," Bet said. "Not in the long term."

"Bet." Cordelia squeezed her hand. "If you knew the wretched mess Harry and I made of our relationship, you'd be much more confident of the future."

"You're very kind," Bet said. "But it couldn't possibly work. We're so different."

"Oh," Kitty said, "all of us are. Different from our partners, that is. If you knew how often Julien and I—"

"No, it's not like that. That is, it is, but more. We don't speak the same language. Not really." Bet's fingers dug into the figured silk of her skirt. Mélanie remembered taking Bet to her modiste to order that gown and the way Bet had cautiously fingered the bolt of fabric when Marthe took it from the shelf. "You've been very kind about helping me learn the right things to say, and what words mean that I didn't know, and when to sit and stand and curtsey, and which fork and knife to use when, and when I went to St. Giles tonight I realized how much my accent has changed. But even so—there are times Sandy and I are laughing together and then he suddenly says something I completely don't understand. Or he's with his friends—even some of you—and suddenly they're talking about something and I know the words, but it's a language I can't begin to understand."

"Sweetheart." Mélanie set down her coffee and touched Bet's arm. "That happens with Malcolm too. I used to tell him he'd never be able to see past being a British gentleman, and he'd accuse me of not giving him credit for seeing beyond the confines of his world. And he was right. He sees the world in a far more complex way. But there are still moments when he says something to a childhood friend—even to Cordy"—Mélanie glanced across the silver coffee service at her friend, who gave a smile of acknowledgement—"and they're in a completely different world. It's not a world Malcom particularly wants to be in."

"It's not one Cordy wants to be in either," Cordelia murmured. "Not most of the time. And I'm quite sure Malcolm doesn't care about it or even miss it."

"No," Mélanie agreed. "He'd say he left it behind long ago. But the truth is he can't entirely, and at times he slips back there. He may even enjoy it, for a moment. I wouldn't deny it to him. I always get him back. Or rather, he always comes back. It's not a world he wants to live in."

"Julien's the same way," Kitty said. "He can convincingly be a man—or a woman—from every background imaginable. And then suddenly he tosses a quip at someone or responds to a joke I don't understand, and he's a Mallinson and an earl's son. And I'm not."

"Even though your name is Mallinson," Simon said.

Kitty gave a wry smile. "Quite. And don't think I don't realize how fortunate I am that we're able to choose to share a name. It has its uses."

"And its burdens." Simon returned her smile. He had lived with Julien's cousin David for over a decade, far longer than Kitty had been married to Julien, and yet Simon and David were only friends as far as the world was concerned. "I'm rather grateful not to have to decide whether or not to be a Mallinson. Though I can't deny it would be convenient." He settled back on the sofa beside Kitty and took a drink of coffee. "As similar as David and I are, being a Mallinson is a part of him I'll never completely understand. Not on the inside."

"Exactly," Kitty said. "Of course, I'll never fully understand what it's like to be the grandson of a slave either. But then there are plenty of things I've been through that Julien will never fully understand, not on the inside. The same for you and David, or Mélanie and Malcolm, or Laura and Raoul, or Cordy and Harry, I imagine."

Laura nodded. "The trick is listening and trying to understand the best one can, even if it's not one's experience. Goodness

78

knows there are times Raoul slips away from me into the world of spycraft."

"You're part of that world now," Bet said.

"Perhaps, in a way. But there are also times he slips into a past I'll never share."

Mélanie met Laura's gaze for a moment. Arabella Rannoch's ghost hovered in the room. Mélanie knew just how much her friend struggled at times with echoes of Arabella, though Laura rarely mentioned the other woman. Just as she rarely alluded to Mélanie's own past with Raoul. "Smiling and laughing helps at those moments when you realize how different your worlds are," Mélanie said. "Because underneath it doesn't change all the things we have in common."

Bet twisted her hands together. "Sandy and I don't have things in common."

"Don't you?" Kitty asked. "You both like to ice skate and dance. You both like children. You both love music and the theatre. I've seen you laugh at the exact same moment Cherubino hides in *Le nozze di Figaro* and cry at the same lines in the tomb scene in *Romeo & Juliet*. From what I've seen, you have more in common than half the couples in Mayfair."

Bet's brows drew together. Then she shook her head. "No one would ever see us that way. You know how we're looked at when we're out together with anyone but our friends."

"That gives entirely too much power to people whose good opinion shouldn't matter to you at all." Mélanie pulled her shawl round her shoulders. The silk and cashmere were soft beneath her fingers, finer than anything she'd possessed at one point in her life. "Not that I haven't done precisely the same myself. For years after I married Malcolm, I was looked on as a foreign adventuress. Malcolm couldn't understand why I couldn't ignore it. I couldn't understand it either. But it rankled. I suppose it still does, in a way."

"And I'm still the Spanish widow who snagged Lord Carfax,"

Kitty said. "Not that there isn't plenty of gossip about Julien, not that he doesn't feel like an outsider himself at times. But I certainly am. I told myself when I agreed to marry him that I wouldn't let it matter. But I'd be lying if I said it never does. Thank goodness I didn't let it stop me from marrying Julien, though. That would have been a sad waste." She took a sip of coffee. "Or do you think I was wrong?"

"Wrong how?" Bet asked.

"To marry Julien."

"Goodness no. I can't imagine you not together."

"You have considerably better imagination than I did for several months of our relationship. In fact, as little as a week before we married, I'd have said you and Sandy stood a much better chance of marital bliss than Julien and I did."

Bet's cup tilted in her fingers. "There's no question of Sandy's and my marrying."

"Until the moment Julien proposed, I'd have said the same about us. In fact, I thought it for several minutes after he proposed. I'm still rather amazed I came round. I'm not sure if it's a sign of strength or weakness. Or mad hopeless love of the sort I theoretically don't admit exists. At least, I didn't admit it before tumbling into it without realizing what was happening to me."

"I certainly didn't," Mélanie said.

Bet shook her head. "That isn't what Sandy wants. And even if he did, I wouldn't drag him into it."

"I'm not sure you'd be the one doing the dragging," Cordelia said.

"You know what I mean. I couldn't do that to him. Even if he wanted it, which he doesn't. He's never given any indication that he does. But I don't want to be his mistress when he has a wife. I don't think he'd even want a mistress."

"I understand," Simon said in a quiet voice.

Bet's gaze shot to his, at once shy and filled with understanding. "But David wouldn't want to marry anyone. That's obvious—"

"More so to you than to others," Simon said. "But yes, I think you're right. Now."

"I don't think Sandy would want to marry anyone he wasn't in love with," Cordelia said. "That sounds very romantic for me. But then I talk and think much more romantically than I used to."

Bet looked down at the embroidered reticule in her lap. "That's just it. I think I may have to leave him so he can—so he can fall in love properly."

"I'm not sure one can fall in love improperly," Kitty said. "Though Julien would probably claim falling in love improperly is much more fun."

"Julien's rather slow. He didn't understand love in the least until he met you," Mélanie said.

"David's father thought the same about my leaving David," Simon said.

"Yes, but—" Bet bit her lip. "I mean, David wasn't going to fall in love with someone else. That is, not with—"

"A woman?" Simon said. "Probably not. But I'm not sure Sandy is going to fall in love with anyone who isn't you. More to the point, I'm not sure that he should be encouraged to do so."

"Yes, but—" Bet bit her lip. "There's no way forwards for us."

"That all depends on your map-making. For years I thought there wasn't a way forwards for David and me. I confess I'm quite glad to be proved wrong." He clinked his coffee cup to Bet's. "Perhaps you need to chart a new route."

"Do you think there's any chance he'll stop?" Sandy asked Raoul.

Raoul turned to look at Sandy in the tallow light that spilled from the taverns and gin shops lining the street in front of the Green Dragon. "I very much doubt anything will stop Alistair Rannoch. But I think he realizes he can't manipulate you as easily as he thought."

Sandy nodded, eyes dark smudges. "So it didn't do any good."

"On the contrary. It's always good to stand up to tyranny."

"That's O'Roarke." Sam glanced up and down the street. "Never miss a chance to argue for revolution."

Three young men, silk hats askew, staggered out of a tavern and pushed past them. Grunts came from an alley to the left. A couple were using it for what might be called a trysting place, save that the woman was probably being paid. Raoul saw Sandy's mouth tighten and was sure he was thinking of Bet.

Harry cast a sidelong glance at Sandy. "We have more evidence. That will help. And you're going to be dealing with Rannoch for the foreseeable future, Sandy. You staked out a position in a long chess game."

"He can threaten me all he wants," Sandy said, as they turned a corner into a darker side street. Most of the shops were shuttered, though shouts and laughter echoed from the adjoining streets. "I won't have him threatening Bet."

"Even if he does," Sam said, "we won't—"

A figure lunged from the side and grabbed Sam. Raoul spun round and kicked Sam's attacker's legs out from under him.

"Don't move," a hoarse voice said from across the street. "I've got your friend."

Another man had an arm wrapped round Harry's throat. The moonlight caught the knife held to his neck. Sandy had gone still. Raoul met Harry's gaze. Harry curled his hand to show three fingers. Raoul inclined his head a fraction of an inch. On a count of three, Harry elbowed his attacker and spun away. Raoul rushed forwards and knocked the attacker into the wall behind them. Sandy grabbed a stick and swung it at Sam's attacker.

"We don't know anything," Sam's attacker yelled as Harry's attacker slid to the ground. "Just hired to give you a warning."

"Hired by who?"

"Gentry cove. At the Green Dragon."

Sandy bashed the stick against the cobblestones. "In other words, my father just hired people to attack my friends."

CHAPTER 12

"You're sure you aren't hurt?" Bet said for the third time, looking at Sandy, who had pulled a straight-backed chair up beside the settee where she was sitting with Mélanie in the Berkeley Square library. Her gaze was trained on him as though it took all her willpower not to fling her arms round him. Mélanie had had many similar moments with Malcolm.

"None of them got near me," Sandy said. "Lucan got grabbed and Davenport had a knife pulled on him."

"It's not the first time it's happened to him. And I'm sure it won't be the last." Cordelia leaned against her husband, who was perched on the arm of her chair. She looked round the group gathered in the library. Malcolm, Mélanie, Kitty, Julien, Bet, Laura, Simon, Harry, Sandy, Raoul, and Sam. "So the whole point of the shooting wasn't to attack Wellington at all?"

"It appears that way," Raoul said. "We'll see if we can hunt down McCandless, but we wanted to update you first."

"Who was the man who was shot?" Bet asked. "I don't even know his name. How dreadful I didn't ask."

"Understandable," Malcolm said. "It's John Bennet. He owns a hotel in Bloomsbury."

"Bennet's." Laura looked up from refilling the coffee cups. "I stayed there with my father over twenty years ago when we came to India from England. They were very friendly. It's not Mivart's." She glanced at Raoul, who had once made Mivart's his London home-away-from-home. "Or the Pultney, or anywhere else like that. But it was a place families without a London abode could put up in comfort."

"It still is," Kitty said. "I stayed there with the children when I first came to London."

"I climbed in through the window more than once," Julien murmured. "And also up the backstairs." He glanced at his wife. "Sorry. Not a surprise to anyone, I shouldn't think."

"Hardly, darling." Kitty reached for his hand. "We didn't even do a very good job of hiding it from our friends then."

"Is that why the League targeted Mr. Bennet?" Bet asked.

"I sincerely hope not," Julien said.

"No." Bet colored. "I mean, not precisely. But could it have been because of something he knew about you?"

"I wouldn't think so," Kitty said. "I never met him. A Mr. and Mrs. Elliot were the proprietors when we stayed there. I think Mrs. Elliot is Mr. Bennet's daughter." She looked at Julien. "Did you ever talk to Mr. Bennet?"

"I never talked to any of them. I was doing my best to blend into the woodwork and not bring scandal down on the woman I —on you."

"You've never been worried about scandal in your life, Julien."

"Not on my own account. I didn't want to bring it down on you and the children. It was quite a relief when you got the rooms in Carnaby Street and we didn't have to skulk about quite so much. I do remember overhearing Mrs. Elliot talking to two of the maids once when I slipped in disguised as tradesmen. She struck me as remarkably decent and fair-minded."

"She was very kind to the children," Kitty said. "It occurs to me we should have thought more about the scandal we might have been bringing down on *them*."

"The children or the Bennets?" Julien asked.

"The Bennets. The children were fine. And we were quite discreet."

"More so than I've ever been before. I should have realized I was changing. While it's true I can be wrong about such things, I don't think the Elliots or Mr. Bennet would have recognized me. And even if they had, I can't imagine anything about my being there that would have made anyone attack Mr. Bennet."

"Could Mr. Rannoch—Alistair Rannoch have stayed at Bennet's?" Bet asked.

Malcolm frowned, then glanced at Julien. Julien frowned as well. "I have no reason to think he did. The only times I saw him were outside London, but that was over a year ago. Gelly's never told me where he was staying." His gaze swept the company. "Truly."

Mélanie picked up Berowne, who had jumped up on the settee between her and Bet. "There was a time when I couldn't have imagined saying this to you, Julien, but I believe you."

"He has to have stayed somewhere in London," Laura said. "Bennet's is the sort of anonymous hotel he might have sought out. Though he seems to have enough allies I'm surprised he didn't stay with one of them. And presumably, if he stayed at Bennet's, he'd have known he'd be seen. He'd have to have some specific reason to target Mr. Bennet."

"Assuming the League are behind this," Julien said. "Though it seems by far the likeliest explanation."

"I told Rannoch—Alistair Rannoch—he doesn't have a prayer of even talking to me if he doesn't pull back." Sandy stared at his hands, then looked up, his gaze sweeping the group. "I don't have a lot of faith that will help. But I don't have any faith that he'd do as he said if Bet did go along with what he asked."

Bet nodded. "It was foolish of me to think he would. That doesn't mean—" She shook her head. "Robby's what matters now."

"With Charlotte Somerset's evidence, can you get the charges withdrawn?" Sandy asked.

"We're trying," Malcolm said. "Roth's talking to Nathaniel Conant and he has people looking for McCandless. Though Raoul and Sam may have a better chance of finding him."

"I have some sources from my military intelligence days I can try," Harry said.

"And I'll talk to the other Levellers and see if anyone else was there and saw anything that might help," Simon said.

"I should see what Uncle Hubert has discovered." Julien pushed himself to his feet and held out a hand to Kitty. "Come with me and make sure I don't strangle him?"

Kitty took his hand and got to her feet. "Of course. Much as I sympathize with the impulse, he really does have his uses. Especially at times like these."

BENNET'S HOTEL was in a terrace house in Bedford Place. The Doric portico gave onto a well-proportioned entrance hall with a graceful walnut console table supporting a crystal bowl of roses. The smell of lemon oil hung in the air. As Laura and Kitty had said, it was not the sort of hotel that catered to visiting royalty like the Pultney or Grillion's or Mivart's, but a comfortable, respectable place where families up from the country for a brief sojourn could stay without fear of scandal. Where Laura's father, Colonel Hampson, had stayed when he came from India with his young daughter. Where Kitty had been able to stay respectably as a widow with three young children. The sort of establishment Malcolm had looked for when they fled to the Continent two years before, seeking not to attract notice.

A footman conducted Malcolm and Mélanie to a sitting room

in tasteful stripes of cream, brown, and beige. A short time later, Anne Elliot came into the room. She was a slender woman with thick, dark blonde hair worn in a low knot, level brows, and a thin face. Her blue eyes were shrewd and just now looked tired. "Forgive me," she said. "It's a difficult time."

"Thank you for agreeing to see us, Mrs. Elliot," Malcolm said. "How is your father?"

"Comfortable, thank you. The doctor gave him a large dose of laudanum. But he's hopeful my father will make a complete recovery." She seated herself in one of the tan-and-cream striped chairs, as though she had just realized Malcolm could not sit again until she did so. "I understand you are involved in the investigation into the man who shot at the duke?"

"Yes," Malcolm said. "But we now have reason to believe the duke may not have been the target."

"Who—" Mrs. Elliot stared from Malcolm to Mélanie. "You can't mean my father?"

"The man who was hired to do the shooting wouldn't have missed," Mélanie said.

"They have the man who fired in custody."

"They may have the wrong man," Malcolm said.

Mrs. Elliott shook her head. "Why would anyone shoot at my father? He's the most harmless man imaginable."

"Had he gone to Apsley House to protest?" Malcolm asked.

Mrs. Elliot drew back a little in her chair. "He's been very concerned about the queen. He sees her as ill-used."

"A number of people do," Malcolm said with a smile. "Myself included. Henry Brougham is a friend of mine. Had your father encountered any controversy over his support of the queen?"

Anne Elliot shook her head. "Truth to tell, most people we know support her as well. And it's not as though my father is leading protests. The very idea would make me laugh, if this weren't so serious. He went along tonight because a friend of his asked him."

"What friend?" Mélanie asked.

"A Mr. Jenkins. They met in a coffeehouse and got to talking about the queen's situation. Which is hardly surprising. If one walks into nearly any coffeehouse these days, that's what half the people are talking about. In truth, I can scarcely walk through our entry hall or any of our sitting rooms without hearing her case mentioned."

"Did you ever meet Mr. Jenkins?" Malcolm asked.

"No." Her brows drew together for a moment. "But that's hardly surprising. I've been busy with the hotel and the children, and Papa had spoken with Mr. Jenkins when he was out."

Malcolm nodded. "Does your father have any enemies that you know of?"

Mrs. Elliot drew back in her chair. "That would be laughable as well, if he weren't lying injured upstairs. I know it probably sounds as though I'm a fond daughter making excuses, but the staff loved him."

"We've heard the same from people who've stayed here," Mélanie said. "Had you had any hotel guests who had been difficult? Or who acted suspiciously?"

"We're a very quiet hotel, Mrs. Rannoch. Our guests like it that way."

"Perhaps we could have a look at the registry?" Malcolm said.

"In search of what?"

"Anything that might stand out."

Anne Elliot drew in and released her breath and put a hand to her smooth hair. "Do you have an idea of who is behind this?"

"No," Malcolm said. Which was true. More or less.

Mrs. Elliot nodded, but her gaze lingered on Malcolm's for a moment.

"What did your father do before he had the hotel?" Mélanie asked. "Or did your grandparents start it?"

"Oh no. Papa was born in Argyllshire. He started as a footman. He got a gift from his employer that let him leave service and

89

marry my mother and buy an inn in London and then eventually start the hotel. He's often said how fortunate he was."

"Who was your father footman to?" Malcolm asked in an easy tone.

"Lord Glenister."

The pieces of the puzzle broke apart and reformed into a different pattern, as happened so often during an investigation. "The present Lord Glenister?" Malcolm said.

"Oh, no. The present Lord Glenister's father."

Malcolm shot a look at Mélanie, quick, but as always, they could say a lot in a quick exchange of glances. "When did your father leave the Glenisters' service?"

"Over thirty years ago. Thirty-five now, I think."

"Does he still communicate with the present Lord Glenister?"

"They were hardly friends. Or even what one might call acquaintances. As I'm sure you must appreciate, Mr. Rannoch, the Glenisters have so many footmen my father would have been little more than a name to the family. But the present Lord Glenister has stopped by the hotel on a few occasions and dined here once or twice. I know my father appreciated it."

Glenister could be kind when he put his mind to it. Or when it suited his purposes. Malcolm was more sympathetic to him of late, but he knew better than not to be wary with the man who had been Alistair Rannoch's friend and helped found the Elsinore League.

"Do you know the present Lord Glenister?" Anne Elliot asked.

"He's my godfather."

He saw a flash of appraisal in her eyes. "So you know him well."

"I'm not sure anyone knows Glenister well. Certainly not me. But it sounds as though he and your father were on good terms?"

Anne Elliot hesitated. "I'd say they were cordial. My father was polite, of course. Glenister was polite. His very coming here would be considered a mark of condescension. One wouldn't have expected them to be friendly. Not like two gentlemen from the same circles. But I'd say—" She hesitated, fingers working over her fawn-colored skirt. "Perhaps I'm too imaginative. My sister used to say I read too many novels and they went to my head. But watching my father and Lord Glenister, I had the sense there were things they were both trying not to say."

"A quarrel they were trying to cover up?" Mélanie asked.

"No. Not precisely." Mrs. Elliott pushed a strand of hair into the seemingly flawless knot at the back of her head. "More secrets they were both trying not to allude to. Secrets they knew would be dangerous to both of them." She drew a hard breath. "It sounds like nonsense when I put it into words. I wouldn't speculate like this under normal circumstances. But if someone really did try to harm my father, I want to tell you anything that might possibly help."

"Quite right," Malcolm said.

"I imagine you wish to speak with my father."

"When he wakes and is able to have visitors, we'd be most grateful if we could talk to him." Malcolm cast a glance at Mélanie and pushed himself to his feet. "Meanwhile, it seems I should call on my godfather."

CHAPTER 13

*J*ulien held the door of his uncle's study open for Kitty, then closed it for the second time in one night. Which was one and possibly two visits more than anyone should have to have with Uncle Hubert in four-and-twenty hours.

Hubert was back at his desk making notes, a cup of coffee beside him. He looked up and pushed his spectacles up on his nose. "Oh, Kitty, good. Glad Julien has you to keep him in line."

"That's why I asked her to come with me." Julien strode to the desk. "Well?"

Hubert set his pen down on the ink blotter. "It wasn't easy. But I spoke with Sidmouth and Conant. And with Castlereagh, who'd been with Wellington, along with the PM."

"And? Where was the pressure coming from?"

Hubert reached for the silver coffee pot on a tray on the console table behind him, poured two more cups of coffee, held one out to Kitty, and pushed the other across the desk to Julien. "A source we've dealt with before. So perhaps not entirely unexpected. Lady Shroppington."

Julien whistled.

Kitty went still in the midst of taking a sip of coffee. "What the devil is her connection to the League?"

"I would very much like to know." Julien looked at his uncle.

Hubert added more coffee to his own cup. "So would I."

Julien slammed his cup and saucer down on the desk, spattering coffee on the gilded green leather of the blotter. "You really don't know more?"

"I'm flattered by your conviction that I know more than you, Julien. But surely you realize that isn't always the case."

Julien folded his arms across his chest. "You're almost two decades my senior. You've known her longer. Surely you've acquired some information?"

Hubert took a drink of coffee. "I had no reason to be suspicious of Lady Shroppington. My network may be extensive, but not enough so to acquire information on every dowager in Mayfair."

Kitty tugged a handkerchief from her sleeve and blotted up the spilled coffee. "Serves you right for underestimating women, sir."

"Quite possibly, my dear. You'd think working with you and against Mélanie would have taught me my lesson."

Julien pressed his hands down on the desk and leaned towards his uncle. "You're saying Lady Shroppington pulled the wool over your eyes?"

"Rub it in."

"I'm not doing anything of the sort. I'm questioning if you're telling the truth."

Hubert sat back and met Julien's gaze. "Why would I lie about Lady Shroppington?"

Julien straightened up, gaze not leaving Hubert. "Let me count the ways."

"What does she have on Lord Sidmouth and Sir Nathaniel?" Kitty asked. "Blackmail or the pull of friendship?"

Hubert tented his fingers together. "I'm not sure, precisely.

Perhaps a bit of both. She's friendly with a number of powerful people. No one wants to displease her."

"So the League are definitely behind Robby's arrest," Julien said.

"So it would seem."

Julien reached for his coffee and tossed down a swallow. "Can you get him out?"

"We're going to need to give Sidmouth proof. Or at least a probable alternative."

"We've done that. Malcolm and Mélanie got Fitzroy and Harriet Somerset's daughter to write out a statement about where the shot came from."

Hubert frowned. "She's younger than Colin and Leo and Timothy."

"She's five, which means she probably has sharper ears than any of us," Julien said. "What's more, Wellington's prepared to back her up."

"She's still a child." Hubert tugged a paper out from under his coffee cup. "That gives Sidmouth and Conant cover to bow to Lady Shroppington's pressure. It rather depends on how much pressure she can exert."

"Was Lady Shroppington Alistair Rannoch's mistress?" Kitty asked. "Is she?"

Hubert smoothed the edges of the paper. "I've never been privy to a list of Alistair Rannoch's mistresses. Certainly, stranger things are possible than his having a mistress twenty years older."

Kitty folded the coffee-stained handkerchief. "But there are reasons other than romantic love for a woman to seek power. In fact, love, so called, is often a way of seeking power."

"So it is." Carfax reached for his cup and took a sip. "I'm not in a position to comment on Lady Shroppington's motivations."

"It appears we all need to become more familiar with her motivations," Julien said. "Considering she's one of our major opponents."

"Our?" Hubert asked.

"Assuming you're telling the truth about being our ally against the League." Julien clunked his cup back on its saucer. "But of course—"

He broke off at the opening of the door. Amelia Mallinson, his aunt, came into the room. She hesitated a moment on the threshold. "Julien. Kitty. It's good to see you here." Her gaze moved to her husband, cool and level. "I'm sorry to interrupt, Hubert, but a note was delivered from the prime minister. I thought you'd want to see it, and it was better I came in than one of the footmen."

"You have unerring instincts, my dear." Hubert smiled at his wife and held out his hand. Amelia put the note into it. She stayed out of the spy business, from everything Julien could tell, but he was also quite sure she was aware of far more than she let on. And that Hubert knew it. But the easy understanding between them had been strained by the revelation that Hubert was Gisèle's father. The unstated cooperation was still there, but he could feel the knife edge beneath it.

Hubert slit the seal and scanned the note. "Liverpool wants to see me. He's had the report from Wellington about Charlotte Somerset's testimony."

"And he's still facing pressure from Lady Shroppington," Julien said.

"Very likely."

"Lady Shroppington is involved in this?" Amelia asked.

"Do you know her, Cousin Amelia?" Kitty said.

"One can scarcely fail to know her," Amelia said. "She was already a fixture in society when I made my debut."

"She's causing difficulties," Kitty said. "Difficulties that could put Robby Simcox in Newgate."

Amelia frowned. "The brother of the young woman Sandy Trenor is entangled with?"

"Yes. He works for Julien. And Lady Shroppington and others are trying to use Robby's plight to separate Bet and Sandy."

95

Julien had the greatest respect for Kitty's instincts. But bringing up Bet and Sandy with his aunt seemed to be playing with fire. Yet Amelia pursed her lips. "I was surprised Alexander brought her to your ball. But they seem sincerely attached. Lady Shroppington is the last person who should be interfering in anyone's life."

"What we need," Kitty said, "is leverage we can use against her. Would you happen to have any?"

Amelia's carefully plucked brows tightened. Her face went still. Then she gave a slow smile. "I always hesitate to interfere in Hubert's affairs. But in this case, I believe I can help."

~

"MALCOLM." Frederick Talbot, Marquis of Glenister, pushed himself to his feet when the footman showed Malcolm into his study. "Aren't you supposed to be holed up with Brougham and Denman and the others, strategizing how you'll demolish the case against the queen?"

"I was earlier tonight. We've had unexpected developments."

"You'd better sit down." Glenister waved his arm towards two chairs by the fireplace covered in claret-colored leather, crossed to the drinks trolley, and poured two glasses of whisky. "Given the hour, you might well have found me in bed with someone. In fact, it speaks volumes about the state of my current life that you found me alone." Glenister frowned into the glass in his hand, then handed it to Malcolm.

Malcolm accepted the whisky. The smell of an Islay malt familiar from childhood wafted towards him. "There was gunfire near Apsley House tonight. Near the duke's carriage."

Glenister froze in the midst of picking up his own glass. "I confess I didn't see that coming. I probably should have done, the way things have been going. Who'd have guessed it would take an unfaithful wife to rouse the populace to act like Jacobins."

Malcolm took a sip of whisky. Like Alistair, Glenister had excellent taste in malts. "An unfaithful wife with a very unfaithful husband. And I could write you treatises on how far today's protests are from the French Revolution."

Glenister dropped into one of the chairs and took a drink of whisky. "I hope you haven't roused me from my bed to read me a treatise, Malcolm."

Malcolm moved to the chair opposite. "You haven't asked, but the bullet missed Wellington."

"I assume you'd have told me if he'd been struck. Did it hit anyone else?"

"Yes. A man named John Bennet. I understand he was once employed by your family as a footman."

Glenister's dark brows drew together. "Is he all right?"

"They're hoping he'll pull through."

Glenister turned his glass in his hand. The light from the brace of candles on the table between the chairs sparked off the Glenister crest etched in the crystal. "I remember him as a boy. He was kind. Grew up on the estate. He came to London and started a hotel. Bennet's in Bloomsbury. I've been to see him from time to time."

"Uncle Frederick." Malcolm sat forwards in his chair. "A trained gunman was hired to shoot at Bennet. All indications are the League were behind it. The likeliest reason we can come up with for why they would target him is his connection to your family."

Glenister's fingers froze round his glass. "Are you accusing me of being behind this?"

"No. I think the faction trying to take over the League are behind it. The faction run by Alexander Radford." Malcolm hesitated. Information was power, and sharing each bit was a calculated move in the chess game with the League. But Glenister had become an ally, of sorts.

"I know who Alexander Radford is."

97

Glenister's still fingers turned bone-white. Malcolm had been almost certain Glenister knew the truth about Alistair. Now he had confirmation. "How long have you known?" Malcolm asked.

Glenister's hand jerked to his lips. He tossed down a swallow of whisky. "I had questions from the moment I heard of Alistair's supposed death. I could have believed a carriage accident, but Alistair wasn't the sort who had accidents. Then when you claimed Dewhurst was behind it—I couldn't see Dewhurst's surprising Alistair."

"No, nor could I," Malcolm said. "Not if Alistair was on his guard. That started me wondering even before I knew Alistair was alive."

"How did you learn he was?"

Malcolm took a drink and let the whisky burn a trail down his throat. "Alistair came to see me."

Glenister clunked his glass down on the table with the brace of candles. "What did he say?"

"He wanted to make a deal. Danielle Darnault's memoirs to barter for a royal pardon in exchange for letting me keep what might inaptly be called my inheritance. Or he threatened to reveal certain things about my family."

Glenister's gaze locked on Malcolm's own. Malcolm wasn't sure quite how much Glenister knew about Mélanie and Raoul, but he wasn't going to start running risks now.

"Did you give Alistair the memoirs?" Glenister asked.

"What do you think?"

Glenister inclined his head. "So Alistair is now a threat to your family."

"Presumably. It's a matter of debate among my friends and family how far he'll go. What I'm more interested in is why he wants a royal pardon."

"Presumably for the same reason he disappeared."

"And what might that be?"

Glenister took another drink of whisky. "I don't know."

Malcolm clunked his glass down on the table, spattering drops of whisky on the polished wood. "Damn it, Uncle Frederick."

"Truly, I don't. By the time your fath—Alistair—disappeared, I was practically the last person he'd have confided in. I know he was helping Trenchard with his scheme to become prime minister, but that didn't all fall apart until later."

Malcolm wasn't at all sure Glenister didn't know more, but important as it was to learn what was behind Alistair's supposed death and return, that wasn't what was crucial tonight. "A young man named Robby Simcox has been arrested for the shooting. Falsely."

"Simcox. Isn't—"

"His sister is Sandy Trenor's mistress. Alistair's trying to use Robby's plight to force Miss Simcox to leave Sandy."

Glenister grimaced. "That's not surprising. Alistair always took an interest in young Simcox."

"You've always known he was Sandy's father?"

"Oh yes. He told me. Rather boasted about it." Glenister's fingers stilled as he returned his glass to the table. "And yes, given that Alistair fathered—in the crudest sense of the word—my eldest son, that was more than a bit bald-faced. It was also typical Alistair. He doesn't just like to win, he likes to flaunt the win in his vanquished opponent's face. But it rather struck me how much having a son mattered to him. Of course, it always galled him that his actual heir wasn't his son at all."

The Islay malt bit Malcolm in the throat. "Yes, I know. Now."

Glenister's gaze shot to Malcolm's face, softening as it unexpectedly did at times. "It's not your fault, lad."

"No. It just would have helped me defend myself and others against Alistair if I'd understood sooner." Malcolm reached for his glass and took a quick drink of whisky. "And now Alistair's lost Edgar."

"Are you saying Trenor's a replacement?"

"What do you think?"

"It makes a certain sense." Glenister twitched a shirt cuff smooth. "I've always been rather afraid he'd take an interest in Quen."

"Yes, I was too, more recently. But Quen's too independent now. I think Alistair sees Sandy as someone he can mold. I don't think he's right. Though it puts Sandy in a damnable situation."

Glenister settled back in his chair and crossed his legs. "So this explains the League's involvement in the shooting."

"Not in the least. It doesn't explain why they targeted John Bennet to begin with." Malcolm took another drink of whisky. "Bennet's daughter said John Bennet was able to set up in London with a gift from your father."

"Yes." Glenister reached for his glass and turned it on the table. "Father—valued Bennet."

"An interesting choice of words. Are you saying your father was fond of him?"

Glenister's mouth curled. "My father wasn't the sort to be fond. Not of his servants. Not of his children, if it comes to that."

"And yet he entrusted funds to Bennet."

Glenister shifted in his chair. "Even my father had his quixotic moments."

Malcolm leaned forwards in his chair. "Uncle Frederick. What did your father pay Bennet to do?"

Glenister grimaced, picked up his whisky, took a drink. "I don't know." He turned the glass in his hand. "My father was never much in the habit of confiding in me, and particularly not at that time. He'd cut up stiff over my debts and sent me off to rusticate at the shooting box. At the time, I half thought part of the reason he was so difficult about the debts was because he wanted me out of the way. I always rather suspected Bennet had helped him pay off an inconvenient mistress or find a home for a by-blow. But it's not the sort of thing one particularly likes to contemplate about one's parent."

"If it was a by-blow, it would mean you have a sibling somewhere."

"I daresay I have more than one. My father deplored my behavior, but he had quite an active career of his own."

"A by-blow someone would kill today to conceal?"

"I thought you said the League were behind this."

"I think they are. Presumably if your father had a by-blow there could be some League connection."

"If you're asking if there's someone in the League whom my father cuckolded or whose mother or sister my father seduced— or even who is in fact my father's son—I can't swear it isn't true. But until you raised the idea, it had never occurred to me."

"Can you think of any other reason Bennet would be targeted?"

"I can't claim to know him well, but he always struck me as very decent. Seems to get on well with his daughters, which is something I notice rather more of late than I once would have done."

"His daughter Mrs. Elliot said she had the sense the two of you shared a secret."

"Isn't my knowing he'd tidied up something for my father enough?"

Malcolm nodded. He didn't think he had all of it, but he wasn't going to get more from Glenister. He swallowed the last of his whisky and started to push himself to his feet, then said, "What's Lady Shroppington's connection to the League?"

Glenister's brows snapped together.

"I know she has one. And Julien just told me she's the one pressuring Conant and Sidmouth to arrest Robby Simcox." Malcolm and Julien had quickly crossed paths in Berkeley Square before Malcolm called on Glenister.

Glenister swirled the whisky in his glass. "Lady Shroppington took an interest in Alistair from when he was at university."

"Are you saying they were lovers?"

"She's more than twenty years older than he is."

"Tell me you've never bedded a woman twenty years your senior."

"Point taken. In truth, I never cared much to know what was between Alistair and Lady Shroppington." Glenister tossed down the last of his whisky and stared into the glass. "But whatever it was, it's endured."

CHAPTER 14

*M*alcolm came into the Berkeley Square library to find Julien, Harry, and Mélanie sitting on the hearth rug with the children while Laura, Bet, Sandy, Cordy, and Kitty drank coffee. Bet had Clara in her lap. Sandy was sitting across the sofa table, gaze trained on her face.

"Mummy said we could get up because so much is going on," Colin said, dragging a string along the floor for Berowne.

"It's not as though you were going to sleep," Mélanie said.

"And they're excellent at keeping up spirits," Bet said.

Julien looked up from building a fort with sofa cushions. "There's something for you in your study."

Malcolm took a cup of coffee and went into the study to find his sister sitting at his desk. He released a breath he seemed to have been holding since he'd walked into the Berkeley Square library to see Alistair Rannoch. "I've been wondering when I'd see you."

Gisèle swung her gaze to him. "Julien and Mélanie know I'm here. I thought it was better not to get the children excited."

"Yes, I can see that." Malcolm took a drink of coffee and held the cup out to her. He'd seen her little more than a month ago. But

103

that month spanned a world of changes. He hadn't known then that Alistair Rannoch was still alive. Or that Alistair was the focus of Gisèle's undercover work against the League.

Gisèle hesitated, then pushed herself to her feet and took a determined step forwards, the way she'd done since she was a child when she was facing up to something. She accepted the coffee and took a sip. "Julien got word to me. I was already in London. Well, close to London."

"Ian and Andrew—"

"They're with me. Andrew's with Ian now. It's all right, I'm not neglecting my son. Or letting my marriage fall apart."

"I never said you were."

Gisèle took another drink of coffee and held the cup out to him. "No, you have other things to accuse me of."

Malcolm accepted the cup. "I haven't accused you of anything."

"But I can imagine what you're thinking."

"Can you?" Malcolm studied his sister over the steam curling from the cup. "I knew you were brave, Gelly. Now I know just how brave."

Gisèle drew in and released her breath. "I couldn't—"

"There are always choices, Gelly. I'm not saying I agree with all the choices you've made. But I understand they were damnably hard."

"They're not the choices you'd have made."

"I don't always agree with my own choices, on reflection. Or at least I second-guess them. And you have more data in this case than I do." Malcolm studied his sister's determined face. The bones seemed to sharpen whenever he saw her. As though she were emerging from girlhood. Also possibly that she wasn't eating properly. He remembered how thin Mélanie had got at the time of Waterloo. Only in retrospect, knowing what she'd been going through, did he understand why. "I think perhaps you understand Alistair better than any of us."

Gisèle hunched her shoulders. "I don't know that I understand him at all."

"But a part of you is fond of him."

"No—yes, I suppose. In a way." Gisèle chewed on her lower lip. "When I was a girl, I was fond of him. He was kind to me. More consistently than Mama." She picked at the braid on the cuff of her dark blue spencer. "I remember feeling guilty, because I saw the way he treated you and Edgar. I knew it wasn't fair he was kinder to me. Part of me thought I shouldn't like him because of it." She looked up and met Malcolm's gaze. "But I still did."

"You had enough to contend with yourself without worrying about Edgar and me."

"You don't really mean that, Malcolm. Your whole life is built on our responsibility to think of other people."

His eyes must have widened because Gisèle gave a rueful smile. "I do pay attention, you know. Even though I've seemed hopelessly self-absorbed much of the time. Probably still do."

"My dear sister. I've learnt you're very good at seeming things you aren't. I'd have hoped I'd have learnt not to underestimate you." He watched her for a moment. "Has Alistair talked about Edgar?"

Her fingers stilled on the black braid. "He never told me Edgar was working for the League. Perhaps that was his being cautious. A sign he doesn't fully trust me. I think it's far from the only thing he hasn't told me. After Edgar was killed, he told me the truth. That is, that Edgar had been working for him. He said he hadn't felt it was safe for me to know, because I still saw you and, good as I was, you were clever too, and one never knew what I'd give away inadvertently. Which was a way of saying he didn't trust me. He said Edgar had been impulsive. But that—" She hesitated. "That Edgar had impressed him. That he had more backbone than he— Alistair—had thought. But that he wasn't a strategist. Like you."

Malcolm looked away, then back at his sister. "Does he know how Edgar died?"

"He only said the mission failed. He didn't tell me Edgar was trying to kill you—I don't know if Alistair knows that, but I don't think he'd have told me if he did. He's not a fool. I've convinced him I'm still angry at you, but he knows my feelings are complicated." She hunched her shoulders. "And I'm not sure he'd tell me Julien had killed Edgar if he did know."

"He's made no move to get revenge on Julien."

"No. Not yet." She paused again. "Edgar's death did affect him. More than he would have thought, I think."

Malcolm nodded. He didn't trust himself to speak.

"Malcolm?" Gisèle studied him. "If Edgar hadn't been killed, I couldn't ever have forgiven him for trying to kill you and Annabel Larimer. But is there more? The way you've said everything was over with him, even before he died—"

Secrets within secrets. There was so much they shared, but they couldn't share this. For Kitty's sake. For Leo's sake. Especially now he knew Alistair was alive. "Isn't that enough?" he said.

"Yes. I just wondered—You were so very definite."

"What do you think Alistair wants?"

Gisèle frowned, with the attentiveness of one piecing together fragments of code or bits of the historical record. "I think he'd say he wants back what he lost. But I think though he might not admit it that means more than the Berkeley Square house and Dunmykel, his seat in Parliament, control of the Elsinore League. I'm not sure even he could explain what it really means. But I think it's the life he had. What you and Mélanie have that you took with you to Italy. What he never really had at all, in a sense. I think he's destined to be disappointed. But then, I think he always has been."

Malcolm had grown accustomed to his sister's brilliant spycraft. He wasn't as used to her insights into people. He nodded. "I confess for much—perhaps all—of my childhood I was too busy defending myself against him to have any sort of understanding of him." He hesitated. "Does Andrew know about Alistair?"

"Yes, but I only just told him. I wanted to tell him sooner. But I wasn't sure he could manage to keep it from you. He's become amazingly adept on missions, but to keep a secret like that from one of his oldest friends—And then, I wasn't sure he'd agree that we *should* keep it. I was starting to have to fight with Julien about that."

"Understandably."

Gisèle lifted her chin. "What would you have done if we'd told you, Malcolm? Gone on living your life, in the house that was Alistair's, as though nothing had changed?'

"The house is Alistair's."

"And if you'd given any hint you knew that, it would have given everything away. Would have put me at risk. And Andrew, and Julien, and perhaps Ian."

Malcolm set the coffee cup down on the desk with a click. "I'm an agent, Gelly. I'm used to dissembling."

"This is different." She fingered a fold of her skirt. "I was afraid it would destroy you."

"I'm not used to being thought so fragile. Though Mélanie and Raoul have the same tendency at times."

"Malcolm—" Gisèle came up to him and gripped his shoulders. "It was hard enough for me. And my relationship with Alistair isn't as complicated. And I wasn't his heir, not to your degree. Though I confess I hate the idea that Dunmykel is his."

"It's a house. It shouldn't matter so much. But yes, I love it. And Berkeley Square."

"I'm glad you can admit it."

He took her hands. "It was a hell of a risk you were running if I learnt the truth. But I can see your thinking you were better—I was better—we all were better off with my not knowing."

"That's quite an admission."

"Well, whatever you did, we have to go forwards from where we are now."

"I think—" Gisèle hesitated. "Alistair understands my feelings about you are complicated. But I'm only just coming to under-stand how complicated his feelings about you are."

"It must have been maddening to have to accept a child that wasn't his. I can't say I'd have reacted the same way, but I do appreciate it was a difficult situation."

"Only you could use the word appreciate about it, Malcolm. But I think it was more than that. You were a living reminder to him. You are a living reminder."

"Of his embarrassment?"

"Of Mama's having loved Raoul."

Malcolm felt his fingers go still over her own.

"You don't think so?" Gisèle said.

"No, I think you're damnably acute, sister mine. Though I wouldn't have put it that way until recently."

"It doesn't excuse anything he's done."

"No. I've learnt one may feel sympathy for people who have done absolutely unforgivable things. It doesn't mean one forgives them. But it may be a key to understanding Alistair. And I think we need to understand him."

"In order to defeat him."

"That depends on what he wants. At the very least, in order to protect ourselves from him."

"You're a diplomat at heart, Malcolm. But can you really see making a treaty with Alistair?"

"If it was the sort of thing where we retreated behind our mutual borders? Yes. But I'm not sure Alistair would accept that."

"Nor am I. That is, I'm quite sure that he wouldn't. Even you must realize sometimes battle is inevitable."

"Sometimes. I'm sorry, Gelly."

"Why?"

"Because it will be hard for you to oppose him."

Gisèle gave a quick laugh. "I've been opposing Alistair ever since I learnt he was alive and I ran off from Dunmykel."

"But this will be more direct. And you've been undercover for over a year. That can change one. Ask Mel."

"Mélanie fell in love with you. I assure you I don't love Alistair in any sense of the word."

She might love her childhood vision of what Alistair had seemed to be, but Malcolm wasn't going to say that. Instead, he said, "I won't discount that, where Mélanie is concerned. But she'd be the first to tell you it was more than that. It was forming friendships, seeing what once had been the enemy as individuals, living in her role so much she came to think like the character she was portraying at times."

"I remember when I first saw Mélanie with you. I'm quite sure she wasn't playing a role."

"Not all the time. But Mel would never have become the perfect diplomatic wife unless she was playing a role."

"And the Elsinore League aren't the same as British society."

"The Elsinore League come from British society. And you play your role so well you must have learnt to think your way into it."

"No. Yes, all right, I suppose so. At times."

"Your persona is grounded in reality."

"It's grounded in who I used to be. I couldn't convince Alistair I was angry at you otherwise."

"I imagine you're still angry at me at times."

"Well, yes. I imagine brothers and sisters are always angry at each other at times."

"Gelly—" Malcolm released her hands and set his own hands on her shoulders. "You have a right to be angry at me for leaving."

"I was a child."

"Which is part of why I shouldn't have left. And children can have remarkably keen instincts."

"Which is why I always knew Alistair was unfair to you. Even when I cared about him. I'm not going to turn on you and support Alistair, Malcolm. I wouldn't. We have enough things to worry about. Don't worry about that."

"Did I say I was?"

"No, but given the people who've betrayed you, it would be wonderful if you didn't wonder. I know where I stand. I know what I believe in."

Malcolm looked into his sister's eyes and nodded. "I rather think you do." He took a step back and folded his arms. "Has Alistair ever talked about Sandy Trenor?"

"No. I only know he's Alistair's son from you. Why—does that have to do with—"

"How much do you know about what's happening tonight?"

"Alistair was planning something. But he didn't tell me the details."

"Robby Simcox has been arrested. For shooting at the Duke of Wellington."

"Good God."

"And Alistair is trying to use Robby's fate as leverage to get Bet Simcox to leave Sandy."

Gisèle frowned. "I suppose it makes a sort of sense. I think Alistair wants family. In a way he never admitted to. He's lost Edgar."

"Quite." Leo was there, a presence he couldn't discuss. For an instant, in his own silence, Malcolm understood Gisèle's silence about Alistair.

"Alistair had the Duke of Wellington shot at for leverage over Bet Simcox?" Gisèle asked. "That seems extreme even for him."

"I'm not sure he was shooting at the Duke of Wellington at all. Another man was shot, seemingly by accident, but we're starting to think it wasn't an accident at all. A John Bennet. A hotel owner who was once a footman to the Glenisters. Does the name mean anything to you?"

Gisèle shook her head. "It seems very odd."

"What about Lady Shroppington?"

"I've never met her. I was telling you the truth about that."

"But at that point I didn't know Alistair was alive. What's the connection between them?"

Gisèle's brows drew together. "I don't know. I don't think she's his mistress. But he respects her opinions. More than he respects most people's. At the same time, he gets angry with her at times. And to be honest, I'm not sure which of them has the upper hand."

"The upper hand in what?"

Gisèle chewed her lip. "To know that, I'd have to know what their goal is."

"Lady Shroppington wants Alistair back in control of the League?"

"Yes. That is—Lady Shroppington and Alistair are allies. But to own the truth, I'm not sure which of them is trying to run the League. And I'm not entirely sure they are. Alistair once complained to me about her 'constant meddling.' But then he said, 'I'm fortunate to have some allies who don't let me down.'"

"The fact that Alistair calls anyone an ally is significant."

"Lady Shroppington is definitely significant. I just can't figure out how."

"How recent is her connection to the League?"

Gisèle pleated a fold of her skirt between her fingers. "I don't think it's recent at all. I think she's been involved in the League from the first."

Malcolm's image of an organization founded by Alistair and Lord Glenister in their undergraduate days spun and fractured in his brain. "She started it—with Alistair?"

Gisèle frowned at her nails against the blue sprigs. "I think she may have started it."

That was another surprise on a night full of them. Malcolm opened his mouth to ask more, when his wife stepped into the room.

"I'm sorry," Mélanie said, "but Mrs. Elliot just sent word her father is awake."

CHAPTER 15

*J*ohn Bennet turned his head on the pillow. He was a handsome man, with a strong-featured face and thick, dark hair little touched by gray. Even lying in a sick bed, he had the sort of dignity Malcolm had often seen in staff members in great houses. A more determined dignity, in many ways, than their employers showed. "It's kind of you to visit me."

"Your daughter says you're feeling better, Mr. Bennet," Mélanie said.

"I'll do, ma'am, thank you. Take more than a bullet to get rid of me." His gaze flickered between them. "I understand there's some question about who fired the shot?"

"There seems to be," Malcolm said.

"Wouldn't want the wrong person arrested. Too much of that's gone on, begging your pardon."

"I understand you worked for the Glenisters," Malcolm said. "Our families were friends." Which was more or less true, though given his own relations to Alistair Rannoch and the nature of Alistair's and Glenister's relationship, it strained both the word "family" and the word "friends." "We visited them in Argyllshire, but I don't remember ever seeing you there."

"I left before you'd have been born, Mr. Rannoch. About thirty-five years ago now." Bennet drew a breath, the sort that covered words unsaid.

"Mr. Bennet—" Malcolm sought for the right words. "We have reason to believe the shot may not only have been fired by someone other than the man who was arrested, but that the target may have been you rather than the duke."

"Me?" Bennet's thick dark brows shot up. "Why on earth would anyone go to the trouble to shoot at me?"

"That's what we're endeavoring to discover. We've been talking to your daughter to see if you may have any enemies." Malcolm smiled at Anne Elliot, who was sitting nearby, not so close as to intrude, but close enough to keep an eye on her father.

"I don't imagine a man gets to my age without angering a few people, but I wouldn't say I have enemies. Never one to hold a grudge, and not important enough anyone would try to get rid of me."

Malcolm cast a quick glance at his wife. So challenging always to know how much to lead a witness. But in this case—"We were wondering if it might go back further. Perhaps to your days in Lord Glenister's service."

He was more than half prepared for another denial, but Bennet's brows drew together. "I told you I left thirty-five years ago."

"Your daughter said the elder Lord Glenister gave you a handsome gift."

"He was kind." Bennet hesitated just a bit over the word, much as Glenister had done.

"Was the gift in recompense for some service you had rendered him?"

Bennet's frown deepened.

"Mr. Bennet," Mélanie said. "Whoever hired the man who shot

you won't stop. Next time your family could be caught up in this. It is imperative we get to the bottom of it."

Bennet's gaze moved to his daughter. She returned his regard steadily. "I'm worried about you, Papa," she said. "And yes, about the children. But even more than that, Mr. and Mrs. Rannoch need to know the truth."

Bennet released his breath in a rough sigh. "It wasn't so very unusual. Dozens of cases like it, and he did see to the child. Always felt sorry for her, though."

"The child?" Malcolm asked, still unclear whose child it was, though so far the story fit with Glenister's suggestion that Bennet had helped conceal an illegitimate child of the senior Lord Glenister.

"No. One hopes the child never learnt the truth. Lady Georgiana."

"Glenister's sister?" Malcolm said. "That is, the present Lord Glenister's sister."

"Yes." Bennet looked at his daughter, though he seemed to have trouble meeting her gaze.

"You can't think I'm shocked, Papa," Anne Elliot said. "And Mrs. Rannoch doesn't look shocked either. As you said, it's not an uncommon story."

"No." Memories clouded Bennet's gaze. "Lady Georgiana found herself"—Bennet coughed—"with child. Barely seventeen, poor girl. Went away to have the baby in secret."

It was indeed not an uncommon story. Mélanie and Julien had helped Hortense Bonaparte in a similar situation.

"Georgiana Talbot didn't marry until several years later," Malcolm said. To a half-pay officer. Malcolm remembered a rare visit she had made to the Glenisters' country house. He had an image of a care-worn woman with graying hair and tired eyes, by then the mother of four or five. She'd seemed old, but had probably been younger than he was now. "The baby was sent away?"

Bennet nodded. "There was quite a hush about it. I was sent to give money to the new family. Not anything one could blame Lord Glenister for. It would have been worse if he hadn't provided for his grandchild. But he never seemed comfortable with me after that. Offered me funds to set myself up in London not long after. Said he knew I'd been wanting to strike out on my own. Which was true. But I couldn't but feel I was being sent away. I felt a bit odd taking the money. Like it was tainted some-how. Paying me off for doing something underhanded. Though at the time I hadn't felt I'd done anything wrong. Didn't stop me from taking it. Without it, I wouldn't have been able to marry Sally or start the hotel." He looked at his daughter again, this time with a smile. "Anne wouldn't have been born, or our younger daughters. Can't say I regret it. But it bothers me when I think back."

"It sounds as though you merely performed a service you were asked to undertake," Mélanie said.

"You're kind, ma'am. I still feel there's a great deal I don't understand about it." Bennet looked at Malcolm. "Not sure I should be telling you this. But then, perhaps you know some of it already."

"What makes you think so?" Malcolm asked.

Bennet hesitated again.

"Mr. Bennet," Malcolm said. "My wife spoke the truth. We need to learn what is behind this. To protect you and your family and get an innocent man released from custody."

Bennet released his breath. "The man Lord Glenister engaged to make arrangements about the baby. It was a friend of his son, the current Lord Glenister. Mr. Alistair Rannoch. I believe he is your father, sir."

Malcolm felt himself go still. "No, as it happens, though I grew up thinking he was. And while I didn't know he had anything to do with Georgiana's unfortunate story, I am not wholly surprised. Do you know who the child's father is?"

Bennet shook his head against the pillow. "I don't believe it was Mr. Rannoch. He seemed to be undertaking a commission for Lord Glenister rather than being personally engaged in the matter."

Alistair would have been quite capable of not appearing—not being—personally engaged if he had been the child's father, but Malcolm didn't press the issue. "Do you know where Alistair Rannoch took the child?"

"Oh yes, sir. That's where I delivered the money. To a couple on the Dunmykel estate. They seemed most respectable. The wife had been with child, so they were able to present the baby as one of a set of twins. I believe their name is Thirle."

Malcolm's fingers went numb against the covers. He felt Mélanie's stillness, though he didn't risk meeting her gaze. "Yes. Mr. Thirle was the estate agent at Dunmykel for many years. They do have twins. A son and daughter. Do you know—"

"Lady Georgiana's child was a boy."

Which meant that Georgiana's Talbot's child, the baby Bennet had helped Alistair hide away, was Andrew Thirle, Gisèle's husband.

ANDREW STARED AT MALCOLM. They were in the Berkeley Square study, where Gisèle had summoned Andrew. Gisèle, Malcolm,and Mélanie were all gathered in the circle of lamplight close to the desk, but right now Andrew's attention was trained on Malcolm. He was Malcolm's oldest friend, but from their boyhood rambles at Dunmykel, their lives had gone in different directions, with Malcolm going to the Peninsula as a diplomat and agent while Andrew read law in Edinburgh and then went home to Dunmykel and became the estate agent after his father. His marriage to Gisèle and Gisèle's undercover work had pulled him into the world of espionage, but he would often still stare at the spies in the group as though he had stumbled into the realm of the faeries.

He also, unlike Malcolm, loved the man he had grown up calling Father.

"I know," Malcolm said. "It's a lot to take in. It must be hard to believe."

"That's just it." Andrew scraped a hand over his thick, dark hair. "I can't say I ever guessed it. Not close. My God, how could I? But it makes sense. I don't look like the rest of the family. Mother's eyes are green, Father's were blue. Her hair is fair, his was carrot-red. You can see them both in Maddie. They're knit up in her. You can see it in her children now. Ian looks like Gelly. He looks like me. But—I'm the cuckoo in the nest."

Gisèle reached for Andrew's hand. "The way one looks doesn't mean anything, darling."

"No." Andrew squeezed her fingers. "But I remember once when I was at university—when I tumbled into helping the local smugglers and my parents found out. My parents were talking late at night, and I heard my father say 'I was always afraid blood would tell.' I couldn't make sense of which of my ancestors he was talking about. I puzzled over it for weeks, then let it go. But looking back—"

Gisèle's gaze fastened on Andrew's face. Malcolm had wondered sometimes of late how much Andrew figured in her calculations, but now she was entirely focused on him. "Your father loved you, darling. That was plain to me for as long as I could remember." She looked down at their son Ian who was asleep with his head in her lap, then back at Andrew. "I used to be jealous of how much both your parents loved you and how much you loved them."

Andrew lifted her hand to his lips and kissed her knuckles. "I loved my parents. I'm glad they raised me. I'm glad Mama is Ian's grandmother. I wish Father had lived to see him. But I'm not surprised. Or I am, but it's as though the pieces of the puzzle have fallen into place." He folded Gisèle's hand between his own and looked at Malcolm. "This man who was shot tonight.

Someone was trying to kill him because he knows about my birth."

"It seems that way," Mélanie said. "At least because he knows something about it."

Andrew shook his head. "Whatever I suspected at the back of my mind about my parentage, I always thought I was on the fringes of—everything all of you are involved in. The League. Missions. What drives all of you. I wanted to do my bit to support my wife, but I thought I was playing a minor part." He touched Ian's hair, then looked at Malcolm again. "Georgiana Talbot is my mother. I mean, she gave birth to me."

"Apparently."

"And she's—"

"She married a half-pay officer. They live in Ramsgate. They have a large family. Six or seven children, I think."

Andrew nodded, gaze fixed. "And my father—at least, the man who sired me?"

"I don't know. Bennet didn't know."

Andrew's gaze shot to Gisèle. "Do you know?"

"Darling. My God, don't you think I'd have told you?"

Andrew gave a rough laugh. "How often have we heard Malcolm and Mélanie, or Kitty and Julien, or Laura and Raoul say that to their spouse? No, I don't think you'd have told me in the least. Not if you thought it would jeopardize me or Ian or the mission or a dozen other things."

Gisèle bit her lip. "Maybe. Depending on what the truth was and what the stakes were. But I don't know." Her brows tightened. "I didn't have the least idea of any of this. I daresay I deserve that you don't believe me, but—"

Andrew brought up his free hand to touch her cheek. "No, I believe you. At least, as much as any of us can believe those close to us."

"Oh, my God," Gisèle said. "What have I done to you?"

"It sounds as though I'd have been in the midst of this regardless of what my wife was involved in." Andrew looked from Gisèle to Malcolm. "Could Alistair be my father?"

Gisèle drew a breath that cut like jagged glass.

"It's a fair question," Andrew said. "The senior Lord Glenister had Alistair intimately involved with his daughter's secrets. The baby's father is one person he might have entrusted those secrets to. It wouldn't make us brother and sister. It wouldn't make us anything by blood."

Gisèle swallowed. "Alistair's never said you're his son. He's never given me any reason to think it. But there's a lot he doesn't tell me. He's never mentioned Georgiana Talbot at all."

"For what it's worth, I doubt it," Malcolm said. "For one thing, Glenister, the current Glenister, appears to have been shocked when Alistair seduced his wife. That seems to be when their relationship fell apart. I suspect it would have fallen apart a lot sooner if he'd known Alistair had seduced his sister."

"It's possible he didn't care much about his sister," Andrew said in an even voice.

"It is. Especially given the man Glenister was then. Or that he didn't know. But more to the point, given the interest Alistair is showing in Sandy Trenor, I suspect he'd be a lot more interested in you if he had reason to think you were his son. Especially given that you're married to Gelly."

"I could handle the news that Alistair is my father. But that's one of many reasons I'm glad he probably isn't. Which leaves the question of who is. And why Alistair would commit murder to cover this up. I mean, it sounds as though what he did was accept money from the senior Lord Glenister to cover up his daughter's indiscretion. Which is scarcely more scandalous than all the things that are publicly known about him."

Gisèle frowned. "Yes, it doesn't make sense. Not knowing Alistair. And yet it seems tied to the other things he's doing now."

"To whatever he's so determined to cover up and get pardoned for?" Andrew asked.

Gisèle nodded. "And I don't know what that is. Truly. Alistair trusts me far more than he should, but he's too clever to trust me completely."

"But you think you can find out," Andrew said.

"I think I have a chance." Gisèle met Andrew's gaze and then Malcolm's and Mélanie's, her gaze at once determined and pleading. "That's why I have to keep working with him. All the more so, now."

Andrew gripped her hand and nodded.

CHAPTER 16

"What's happened?" Bet rushed into the Brown Bear and ran between tables to grip Roth's arm, heedless of the scattered few still seated at the other tables. Kitty and Sandy followed more slowly. Julien closed the tavern door behind all of them. Roth's message had got to them in Berkeley Square while Malcolm and Mélanie were talking to Gisèle and Andrew, about issues Julien did not yet understand, save that he knew they were both urgent and deeply personal, so the four of them had hurried to the Brown Bear, leaving Laura and Cordelia to explain.

Roth caught Bet's hands, an uncharacteristic break from his role. "There's no need for alarm, Miss Simcox. In fact the news is good." His gaze, tired but lightened by relief, moved from Bet to Sandy, Kitty, and Julien. "Sir Nathaniel has informed me that the charges against your brother are to be dropped."

Bet hugged Roth. "When can we take him home?"

"At once. I'd have had him down here waiting for you, but I didn't want him subject to questioning by any of my colleagues."

Bet rushed towards the stairs. Sandy waited a moment, then followed.

"I never thought to be so grateful to Aunt Amelia," Julien said, as he, Roth, and Kitty moved after them.

"She's responsible for the charges being dropped?" Roth asked.

"Apparently. It seems it was our friend Lady Shroppington who was applying the pressure."

Roth's eyes narrowed. He'd already confronted one murder investigation where he'd been quite sure Lady Shroppington was behind the crime but had been unable to charge her. "I probably shouldn't be surprised. And your aunt—"

"She had some information she said she could put to use," Kitty said. "She didn't share what it was with us."

"I'm not even sure she shared it with Uncle Hubert," Julien said.

"But we have cause to be grateful to both of them in this instance," Kitty said. "Amelia was apparently quite touched by Sandy and Bet."

"Clever of you to have realized that," Julien said.

"Sorry darling, it must have seemed a terrible risk. But I saw her watching them at our ball."

Julien squeezed her hand. "Your perceptiveness never fails to amaze me."

Robby turned to them as they stepped into the room where he had been held. Bet had her arm round him, while Sandy hovered off to the side. "I can't thank you enough," Robby said, his gaze going from Julien to Kitty to Roth.

"You should thank your sister and Trenor," Julien said. "They rallied the rest of us."

"Have you found the man who actually did the shooting?"

"I have patrols searching for him," Roth said "But Lucan and O'Roarke and Harry Davenport are likely to find him first, I suspect. Proving he did the shooting will be challenging. Proving who hired him will be harder."

"So it's not over," Robby said.

"Far from it, I'm afraid," Julien said. "But they won't be able to threaten you. Come home and get some sleep. And then you can help us solve the rest."

Robby grinned.

~

"I CAN'T BELIEVE you actually found McCandless," Cordelia said.

"Sam and Nan worked out where he'd have gone to earth." Raoul scrubbed his hands over his face. They were all gathered back in the Berkeley Square library. He looked as tired as she felt, Mélanie thought, taking a sip from what must be her tenth cup of coffee in the past few hours.

"Using information O'Roarke and Davenport got from their contacts," Sam said. He was sitting on the sofa with Nan. "Roth's sent patrols to bring him in."

"Kit thinks he may have found someone who can identify McCandless at the protest," Simon added. "But that won't prove who hired him."

Raoul reached for his coffee. "And even if he talks, I doubt he has names to put to who hired him."

"If he did say it was Alistair Rannoch, no one would believe him," Julien said. "There are a lot of advantages to being thought dead. As I can attest."

Robby, who had been looking a bit dazed taking in everything that had happened since his arrest, sat forwards in his chair. "Bennet, the man who was shot. Alistair Rannoch wanted to get rid of him because of something he knew from the past?"

"So it seems." Malcolm shifted in the Queen Anne chair he was sharing with Mélanie. He wasn't quite ready, Mélanie knew, to share the revelations about Andrew's parentage and Alistair's role. "I think getting rid of Bennet was the original plan, and then they realized they could target you."

"To get at Bet." Robby glanced at his sister, who was beside him on the settee.

"They targeted you and Bet because of me," Sandy said. "It was unforgivable." He was sitting near Bet, but a little apart, as he had all night whenever they were gathered together.

"I don't think Alistair Rannoch will try the same tactic again," Harry said.

"But he won't stop," Sandy said.

"Not until we figure out how to stop him," Kitty said. "In a number of ways."

"Will Mr. Bennet be safe now?" Bet asked.

"I sent guards to Bennet's," Malcolm said. "People we've hired before and can trust. That should protect him for the moment."

"It's like Gerald Lumley all over again," Robby said. He had first gone to work for Julien protecting Lumley from Carfax.

"Bennet's secret seems to be less political than Lumley's," Malcolm said. "But yes."

"So everything is just as urgent as before," Sandy said.

"Robby's safe," Mélanie said. "That's victory enough for tonight." She looked round at the group gathered in their library. "But we're only at the start of a very long game."

"And we're going to need all of us," Malcolm said.

Harry reached across to grip Malcolm's arm. "I usually hesitate to speak for others, but I don't think any of us would be anywhere else."

HARRY LOOKED AT HIS HANDS. "ODD."

Cordelia turned to smile at her husband in their candlelit bedchamber. "Odd?"

"Sandy tonight. Trying to puzzle through his past, and even more so his present and his future."

Cordelia unclasped the pearl necklace she had put on for the opera, a century ago it now felt. "Oh, at Sandy's age who's thinking about the future at all?"

"He was starting to tonight. Starting to realize what he wants with Bet, I think." Harry stared down at his smudged shirt cuff. "It reminded me of how much I could so easily have missed out on."

"As could I." Cordelia moved to his side and slid her arms round him. "As I've said before, life takes us to unexpected and often quite delightful places."

Harry looked down at her, with that look he sometimes got that was at once bone-deep tender and as detached as if he were examining a new artifact. "When we first got married, did you think about children?"

Cordelia frowned. "Only in the sense that I assumed they were part of marriage. But to be honest, I rather vaguely saw them off in the nursery. I didn't assume I'd spend any more time with them than my parents did with me. Did you think about them?"

"Not really. In any more than the theoretical sense. I'd have said I wanted your children because I wanted you. But I'm afraid I didn't think about the children as people at all."

Cordelia nodded. "It was only after Livia was born that I realized I wanted to be a different sort of mother. I never made a conscious decision about it or decided to be a rebel. I simply started doing things differently, because that was what seemed natural to me. Because I loved her and wanted time with her." She studied Harry. "You were very natural with her from the start."

"I was bloody terrified."

"So was I when she was born." Cordelia rubbed her arms. Odd she'd never talked to him about that. It hung between them, those early years of Livia's life when they'd been apart. They didn't shy away from them, but they also didn't dwell on them. She glanced up and met Harry's gaze and saw he was thinking the same thing. "One muddles through." It applied both to parenting and to their approach to the past. "We're rather good at that."

"So we are." He gave a faint smile. "And while I'll never stop being sorry for the time I missed with her, I couldn't be more grateful I had the chance to be a parent."

"Me too." She studied his face. "But it's not a reason to marry someone."

"No. But it can make one think of the future. That's what Sandy was starting to do today." He reached for her hand. "Cordy —I'm sorry I wasn't there when Livia was born."

Her breath caught. "I sent you away."

"I went away."

"Harry—Considering—"

"I didn't know I was her father? I also didn't know I wasn't. And by the time she was born, you were alone. That is—"

"Yes," she said. "I know what you mean."

Harry kept his gaze steady on her own. "Well, then. I could have come back."

"I could have asked you to. But it never occurred to me—oh, devil take it, you know what I mean. We had a long way to go. It was hard to imagine getting back to—anything. Which makes it all the more remarkable that we have done. And makes me distinctly hope Sandy and Bet don't throw away what they have."

Harry reached out and touched his fingers to her face. "They have to recognize what they have first. Which can be damnably hard to do."

"I talked to Alistair," Raoul said.

Laura looked at her husband across their bedchamber. "That must have been difficult."

"It should have been a good chance to learn something."

"Did you?"

"In a way. He told me—" Raoul hesitated. "He loved Arabella enough to want her happiness, even if it meant losing her."

His gaze had slid from her face. "You mean he wishes she was alive and with you," Laura said.

Raoul shrugged out of his coat as though his back was aching. "He thought it might have made a difference if I'd been there. I don't know that it would." He set the coat over the back of the chair at the escritoire, smoothing the shoulders with care. "She tried killing herself when I *was* there more than once."

A hundred different words clogged her throat. Mostly the wrong ones. "I think we've both been through enough in our lives to know one has to find a reason to go on within oneself, not within someone else. From what I've heard, I don't doubt she loved you. But you can't blame yourself. Though I know in your position, I'd do the same."

Raoul gave a twisted smile. "Malcolm asked me once if part of the reason I wanted him to marry Mélanie is that I suspected he wouldn't seek that way out of his troubles again if he had a family. And he's right, to a degree."

"It's a bit different, though. Malcolm, I think, was in despair largely because he felt so very alone and disconnected. So with a family part of what drove him to despair was gone."

Raoul moved to her side and put a hand against her cheek. "You're very wise. Have I mentioned that?"

"I don't know that it's wisdom. It's the perspective of one on the outside. Arabella was different. She was ill, for one thing."

"And her own interests often consumed her. To the exclusion of others. But I'm human enough to think I should have been able to make a difference."

"And you mourn her enough to find solidarity with Alistair's mourning."

Raoul looked straight into her eyes. "I wouldn't have put it in those words, but—yes."

"That's good. I think we're going to need all the ways we can find to make common ground with Alistair."

He set his hands on her shoulders. "That's my Laura. Always assume common ground is possible."

"Better than the alternative." She looked up at her husband. "He's not going to go away, darling."

Raoul pulled her to him and rested his cheek against her hair. But not before she saw the fear in his eyes. "No."

CHAPTER 17

*G*isèle hesitated as she stepped into the study in the quiet, anonymous country house, less than an hour from London, that was Alistair Rannoch's temporary home. So much depended on how she played this. Simplest was probably best. But also most difficult. "I went to see Malcolm."

"I thought you would." Alistair didn't turn towards her, but he held out a hand.

Gisèle moved to the desk. "He'd have come looking for me otherwise."

"What did you tell him?" Alistair turned his head to look up at her.

"As much of the truth as I could." Odd, as Malcolm and Julien had both told her, how the truth could serve, even in the midst of the greatest deception.

Alistair set down his pen and reached for her hand. "I know you care about him. You needn't make excuses."

"You know how angry I've been at him." There, too, she could fall back on the truth. Or at least a version of it.

"You wouldn't be so angry if you didn't care."

"Or at least if I hadn't cared."

Alistair looked down at their linked hands. "You needn't apologize. You're in a difficult position."

"Which is why you don't tell me everything."

"My dear child. I don't tell anyone everything."

Gisèle perched on the edge of the desk. "Malcolm asked me if I understood what you wanted."

"What did you tell him?"

"That I didn't. Not entirely. Which is true. Though I perhaps understand more than I let on."

Alistair sat back in his chair. "Malcolm is a lot of things, but he's no fool. He has to wonder where your allegiances lie as well."

"Putting you both in the same boat?"

"Not a prospect I relish. But perhaps. A bit."

"I don't think Malcolm's come close to working it all out." In fact, she was quite sure he hadn't, considering she hadn't herself.

"Gisèle. Whatever's to come, don't doubt how much your happiness matters to me."

"We're not a family that think much about happiness."

He gave a short laugh. "We're not a family at all, in the larger sense. But you always have been. And always will be."

Guilt stabbed her in the throat again. Damn the man. She should be immune to this. Immune to him. She knew who he was and what he'd done. He threatened everyone she cared about. "Malcolm was a bit distracted. He said Bet Simcox's brother has been arrested."

"Did he say I had anything to do with it?" Alistair's tone was level and easy, offering no hint of what he might know about Robby's having been released.

"He seemed to think you might." Gisèle hesitated. "I think he thinks it's to do with Bet Simcox and Sandy Trenor." She hesitated again, but it seemed to be time to say it. "He says Sandy Trenor is your son."

"Ah. I suppose I should have expected he might. And it was probably past time I told you, in any case."

"So he is."

"According to his mother, and I have no reason to think otherwise. It's difficult, as you can imagine, not being able to publicly lay claim to a child. I should perhaps compare the challenges with O'Roarke."

"And now he's the only son you have."

Alistair's fingers tightened round hers. "I rather gave up on the thought of an heir once I realized the one I had wasn't mine at all. But as time goes on—"

"Children aren't just heirs." Alistair actually seemed fond of Ian. It was disconcerting, but she knew it might prove useful.

"No. I confess I didn't quite realize that until you came along. But one does like the idea of someone to follow one." He looked down at their interlaced hands. "How well do you know Kitty Ashford? Kitty Carfax, I should say."

Dread closed round Gisèle's throat. "What's she to say to anything?"

"Isn't Julien St. Juste's wife rather in the middle of everything?"

"I suppose so, in a way." Gisèle forced her voice to stay even. "I don't think Julien tells her everything."

"Why do you think he married her?"

Gisèle considered a number of answers, and as often decided to fall back on the truth. "I think he's besotted with her."

Alistair gave a short laugh. "That doesn't sound very like Julien."

"He's not the man he was. Though I think he's always been rather different from how he let on. He always seemed rather different to me from how he did to everyone else. Julien used to warn me not to romanticize him, but I'm not really romantic at all. Andrew's the romantic in the family." The mention of her husband brought up all the things she couldn't allude to about John Bennet and the revelations about Andrew's parentage. So much to unravel, so much she couldn't let Alistair guess she knew. Gisèle decided to turn the conversation. "Have you ever

131

met Kitty? She hadn't been in England until a couple of years ago."

"No. I've heard of her but not met her. I've heard she was entangled with Malcolm."

"I think she may have been."

"And Julien's apparently become a doting father to her children."

"Julien's very good with them. As you said, one can suddenly realize what having children means. And I think he likes having the chance to do better than his own father did. Which doesn't seem at all difficult."

Alistair grunted. "That sounds rather straightforwards for Julien."

"Sometimes all of us are straightforwards at unexpected times."

"Perhaps." Alistair tapped his free hand on the desk top. "What about Kitty Ashford?"

"What about her?"

"What does she see in Julien?"

"Will you laugh at me and call me an impossible romantic if I tell you she's besotted with him as well?"

"Probably. From everything I've heard, Kitty Ashford was a very capable agent."

"So was Julien. So is Julien."

"He's an earl, of course. That has to be a lure. But I can't help but wonder whom she's working for."

"Why should she be working for anyone any more than Julien is?"

"Don't think I haven't wondered the same about Julien. But women who go into intelligence are different."

Gisèle's fingers curled inwards. "Different how?"

"Everything is a mission. Look at your sister-in-law."

"I've told you before. Whatever I think of Malcolm, I think Mélanie really does care for him."

"She's a very good actress. So is Kitty Ashford. And they both play a long game."

Which could also be said of her. "If Kitty's playing a game, it's with Julien, not us."

"Probably." Alistair was silent a moment. "How do you think she feels about her children?"

"Most women love their children."

"Don't be naive, Gisèle. Your own mother should have taught you how complicated a woman's feelings for their children can be. And how much or little they can impact her actions."

"Kitty appears to be a very devoted mother. A much steadier mother than Arabella was, actually. No, that sounds dull, and she isn't at all. But I don't think she'd ever go off on a whim, as Arabella did. Or put the mission before her children. The way Arabella did. The way I did." Once again, truth could serve.

"Don't be so hard on yourself, Gisèle. I'm inestimably grateful that you came to see me. And that you sent for Ian."

"I wouldn't do it differently, sir." Another truth.

"I'm glad you aren't so foolish. It doesn't change the question of what Kitty Ashford is up to and how her children might be involved. They play with the Rannoch children, I gather?"

"I believe so. And the Davenports. They're all in and out of each other's houses."

"What about your father?"

Gisèle stiffened. In this there was no need to playact at all. "What about him?"

"Malcolm presumably told him about me. He may no longer officially be Malcolm's spymaster, but they still talk. They still work together. I have no doubt Carfax—Hubert—still has Malcolm doing errands for him."

"I expect he does, but you'll have to ask Malcolm about that and about what he's told Car—Hubert—about you. You can't imagine I have father-daughter chats with him. You'll always be my father." That again was true. She might not be happy that Alistair was her father, she might be working against him, but she would always think of him as her father. For better or worse, he was part of what had formed her.

"No, I suppose not. At least, not all at once. Malcolm seems to quite comfortably think of O'Roarke as his father. But then, I think Malcolm always thought of O'Roarke as his father."

"I think he did without admitting it."

Alistair looked up at her. For a moment his gaze settled on her face, hard and yet at the same time entreating. "That you think of me as your father means a great deal. Never doubt that. But knowing Hubert Mallinson is your father must change the way you view him."

Gisèle forced herself to honestly consider something that she generally buried beneath the exigencies of day-to-day existence. "I suppose so. I mean, I can't look at him precisely the same way. I can't look at him and not think about it—not wonder about the past and if I've inherited anything from him. But mostly I think the people who raise you are more important." So God help her, so far as Alistair had raised her. She hesitated, wondering if she'd damage her role, then decided the comment applied either way. "I expect Sandy Trenor thinks of Lord Marchmain as his father. Even knowing the truth about you, he may not easily be able to change how he views you."

"Not at first, perhaps. But Trenor knows bloodlines matter. They always do, in our world."

"And you still want an heir."

"It's the world we live in. It's the way we tote up the values in our lives."

"Is it true that Quen's your son?"

"I believe so. But I'm hardly going to win him away from Glenister. Glenister appears to have gone amazingly soft."

"Is that what patching up his relationship with his son is?"

"He's gone sentimental."

"And I take it there's more than sentiment to your reaching out to Sandy Trenor?"

Alistair gave a slow smile. "Oh yes. A great deal more."

KITTY DROPPED her cloak on the dressing table bench and stared down at the pile of black velvet. So much settled tonight, so much still up in the air. "Alistair wants to control Sandy Trenor because he's his son."

Julien paused in the midst of removing his cravat, fingers taut on the linen. "So it seems."

"Which might mean he's interested in Leo."

"We don't know that he knows about Leo."

"No." Kitty moved to Genny's cradle, smoothed the covers over her, tucked her stuffed unicorn in beside her. "But we don't know that he doesn't."

Julien tugged the cravat loose and threw it into the laundry basket. "If he tries to do anything to Leo, I'll kill him."

"Julien—"

"I mean it." With barely any inflection, Julien's voice could wield the force of a stiletto slid between the ribs. But of course part of that was simply that he was Julien and one couldn't but be aware of what he was capable of. "Don't think I haven't thought of it in any case."

"I don't think you can make Alistair go away so easily."

"He'd be gone if he was dead."

"It didn't work the first time." A thought occurred to Kitty. She looked at her husband for a moment.

"No, I didn't have anything to do with that," Julien said. "If I had, it would have worked better."

"Even if he were dead, I don't think it would stop what's happening. What the League are after. Or the people trying to control the League."

"I don't know that the rest of them are interested in Alistair Rannoch's descendants."

"Lady Shroppington was the one pressuring Sidmouth and Conant."

"So she was." Julien frowned.

"Julien." Kitty reached for his hand. "That's no answer."

"Sweetheart." He looked into her eyes in one of those moments, rare even between them, when the mask fell away. "I do know that. I'm not the man I was. I don't want to be the man I was. And even then, I didn't—"

"I know."

He lifted her hand to his lips and kissed her knuckles. "Your belief in me is rather staggering. I think I'm supposed to say 'You make me a better man.'"

"If you say anything of the sort, I'll clout you over the head or ask you if you're sickening with something." Kitty looked into her husband's eyes. "Alistair Rannoch is part of Leo's heritage. We're going to have to deal with that at some point."

"Leo shouldn't be tainted by a biological accident."

"It doesn't shape who Leo is. I'll be happier if he never has to learn of it." Kitty locked her arms in front of her. She'd come to terms with Edgar. As much as she ever could. Which wasn't really at all, devil take it. But the threat to Leo had hovered at the back of her mind ever since she'd learnt Alistair was alive. "But with my past, I realize it's better to armor our children against what may happen than think we can wrap them in cotton wool forever."

Julien frowned. "Are you accusing me of doing that?"

The thought of Julien's wrapping anyone in cotton wool seemed nonsensical. And yet—"You treat the children as adults. You're wonderful with them. But when it comes to Alistair, you are protective."

"They deserve a chance to be children."

"Which you never had."

"I don't think you did either. I don't think most of our friends did. Perhaps why we're all making such an effort to do better."

"Don't you think I want them to be children? Leo's growing up too fast as it is." She glanced at the nursery door for a moment. The boys had both been sound asleep when she and Julien looked in on them. "But you should know better than anyone that we have to prepare children for realities they're going to have to face. I thought we had time with Leo. I was afraid when I brought the children to England—it's one reason I wasn't sure I'd stay here—and rather terrified when I learnt Edgar was back from the Continent. But then he was dead, horrible as it was, and I thought perhaps Leo would never have to know."

"He may never have to," Julien said in a low voice.

"Perhaps. The more we learn about Alistair, the more concerned I am. Because it would be ruinous if he learnt it from Alistair."

"He isn't Colin Rannoch," Julien said. "It's one thing to tell a child his biological father is a man he already loves and thinks of as his grandfather, who gets on with his parents with an amity I still marvel at."

"That was difficult enough."

"It was. But they got through it. This is different. It's not easy to wonder how much of one's father may be in one. Especially when one hates one's father."

The quiet savagery in Julien's voice when he talked about his father always shook her, and at the same time made her want to take him in her arms. Kitty touched his face. "There's a lot of you in Leo. And me. That will always be true. More and more, as he grows up. I think we've made him strong enough to realize Edgar can't shape him. Nor can Alistair Rannoch."

Julien's hands settled on her shoulders. "Kitkat—I wish I could have protected you from it."

"I don't need to be protected, Julien. That's the last thing I need or want from you."

137

"I know. Thank God. But you can't blame me for wanting to protect you. Wouldn't you want to protect me in the same circumstances?"

"A fair point." She slid her hand behind his neck. "There's so much I wish I could have protected you from."

"Well, then. You should understand."

"It's the past. It's helped make us who we are, but it hasn't defined us. And I'm damned well not going to let it define Leo."

CHAPTER 18

"I'll talk to Julien about what we learnt from Bennet—about Georgiana Talbot, and Andrew, and Alistair's role—tomorrow." Malcolm tossed his waistcoat over a chair back, after his coat. "I don't think he knows more, but he may have insights. And I need to work out whether to confront Glenister."

"Darling." Mélanie scanned her husband's face, shadowed with exhaustion. "We have time."

"Not a great deal of time. We have to learn why this is so important to Alistair before he uses the information."

"Yes. But he won't use it tomorrow." Mélanie pulled a handful of pins from her hair. "He lost a hand tonight, and according to Raoul, Sandy's standing up to him surprised him. He'll want to think through his next move."

"Which may not take long. He caught us by surprise, moving as quickly as he did tonight. I'm not going to make that mistake again." Malcolm dug his fingers into his cravat and tugged it loose. "Alistair's information about Andrew's birth is one more piece of information he can put to use. He's already threatened to reveal the truth of your past and Raoul's. By now he knows we didn't meet his demands over that. And he'll be even angrier because we checked him tonight."

Malcolm, worried about his family, was at his most stubborn. She loved him for it, even as it drove her to distraction. She pulled more pins from her hair and shook it about her shoulders. "He won't do it, Malcolm. Once he's played that card, he won't be able to play it again. He's too good a tactician to waste it simply in revenge."

"Maybe."

Mélanie went up to her husband and put her hands on his shoulders. "And if I'm wrong and he does try, he can't hurt me or Raoul. But I know it will be difficult for you."

His arms slid round her waist. "I don't give a damn about talk."

"I know, dearest. But you have enough of a battle making your ideas heard in Parliament without your wife's scandal causing a distraction."

"My getting anywhere in Parliament is always going to be difficult given the positions I've staked out."

Mélanie slid her hands behind his neck. "Your wife's being exposed as a former French spy would make it harder."

"I can handle that. I'm concerned about—"

"Protecting your wife. Who doesn't need to be protected."

"My wife has her own career."

"I can write plays in disgrace. If it's not safe for Simon to produce them, I can turn them into novels. Laura and I can write one together."

Malcolm's gaze fastened on her own, level and open. "We could escape. We could be happy. We've proved it. But I don't want to do it."

"Well, no. Neither do I. And I don't think we'll have to." She reached up to kiss him, then drew back. "But I don't like that I've put you in the position where you might have to."

"I've said it before, sweetheart. You gave up far more by staying with me than I've ever risked giving up because of you. Don't make the mistake Bet almost made tonight by thinking differently."

Mélanie saw Sandy and Bet leaving Berkeley Square less than an hour before. Sandy had held open the door, but hadn't given Bet his arm as he usually would. He'd seemed afraid to touch her. "Nothing's really settled between Sandy and Bet. Tonight just made them confront something that was always coming. And now they're going to have to face it."

"Quite. I told Sandy tonight that they can stay with us should then need to."

"Of course. You think his parents are going to cut him off?"

"I think they might, depending on what he does next. I also said that with everything happening in Parliament I'm at the point where I could do with a secretary. Which is true. That would give them an income."

"I love you, darling."

"I hope they can be brave enough not to let conventions or scruples stand in the way of happiness."

Mélanie tilted her head back to look into her husband's shifting gray gaze. "You always accuse me of being the romantic between us. But now you're sounding positively fairytale-like yourself."

A smile played about his lips. "Yes, well, you bring it out in me."

She echoed his smile, but fear tightened her throat. "Sandy and Bet aren't us, Malcolm. We can protect them against Alistair. But they have to sort out what risks they're willing to take themselves."

Malcolm nodded and pressed a kiss to her forehead. "All we can do is try to help them through the consequences."

BET SET her reticule down on the polished satinwood of the dressing table in the bedchamber of Sandy's flat in the

Albany. The aquamarine ring Sandy had given her gleamed on the dressing table, beside her hairbrush and lip rouge. She'd put it there when she'd left for the opera. She'd thought then that she'd never return here. And for all her relief at the night's events, she still wasn't sure how long she could stay.

"Bet." Sandy spoke softly from across the room. "Why didn't you come to me immediately?"

"Oh, Sandy, why do you think?" Bet spun round to look at him. "Grateful as I am that you confronted Alistair Rannoch, I was terrified for you."

"We're supposed to be—we're supposed to share things."

"You've been sharing a lot with me for a long time, Sandy. You've been very generous."

"Generous?" Sandy took a step forwards and then checked himself. After those moments at the theatre, he'd scarcely touched her all night. "Is that what you think this is?"

"It started with your being kind to me."

"Kind?" Sandy scraped a hand over his hair.

"You've been kinder to me than anyone I've known in my life. It's meant a lot—"

"Is that it?" Sandy's gaze fastened on her face. "Is that what I mean to you?"

Bet stared into the eyes she knew so well. "Sandy, you mean everything to me."

"You must know I love you."

For a moment she couldn't move. The words thrummed through her, touching a chord she hadn't known existed. She hadn't realized how much the words would mean to her. Or that she'd be able to believe them.

"I know I haven't said it," Sandy said quickly. "I've never said it to anyone, actually. Not something we say in our family. Stupid to let that stop me. Bet, I can't imagine loving anyone more." He drew a breath. "I'll probably lose my allowance. And the flat. But

Rannoch says he can give me a post as his secretary. And that we can stay with them if we need to."

"Sandy, what are you talking about?"

"What it will be like if you're willing to marry me."

The world spun again. "You can't think—"

"I know it won't be easy—"

"You can't think I'd force you to give all that up."

"You wouldn't be forcing me to give anything up. I'm the one who asked you."

"Sandy. You don't have to do this."

"Of course not. I'm doing it because I want to. Because I love you." Sandy crossed to her side in two strides and seized her hands. "I should have asked you a long time ago. I should have when we first met."

Bet jerked her hands from his clasp. "When we first met—"

Sandy flushed. "I know. I didn't behave well."

He'd been three sheets to the wind, slumming in St. Giles with some university friends. He'd stumbled upstairs with her on a dare and nearly passed out before they were finished. "You were kind. Kinder than most men I'd known."

"I should never—"

"If you hadn't, we'd never have met." And that would have been unbearable, hard as this was now.

He'd been apologetic the next morning. Had insisted on buying her coffee. Had asked, blushing, if he could come back. He'd bowed when he left, a sort of nursery reflex. She'd been charmed and thought she'd never see him again. But he'd come back the next night, with a bouquet of roses. No one had ever brought her roses before. He'd bought her dinner at a tavern that had her favorite pasties. He'd asked her about her family. In and about other activities. Which had also been distinctly agreeable. More agreeable than ever before, actually. She'd been sure the novelty would wear off but determined to enjoy it while she could. Her friends advised her to get as much out of Sandy as she could, but she'd hesitated to even ask him for payment. It cheapened something that she'd never known before. Yet she'd been afraid of taking it too seriously. Every time she saw him, she wondered if she'd see him again, but he kept coming back. And when they were together, sharing tea or brandy beneath a blanket in her room, eating pasties or drinking ale, elbows on a tavern table, talking nonsense or telling stories, it seemed as though they were in their own world, a world they could share, where they were equals and no one else inhabited the space. And then Sandy would mention a ball he'd been to, or a dinner with his parents, or his cousin's debut or a visit to Ascot, and it would come crashing down on her how different their worlds were. And that their shared world couldn't possibly continue.

Until she'd faced danger. Because of Robby, though in the end Robby had proved to be starting to act responsibly for perhaps the first time in his life. But she'd been in danger and Sandy had insisted she move into his flat. Just for a few days, she'd thought. She still remembered the first time she'd stepped into the flat in the Albany. Bachelor quarters, big enough to house three families in St. Giles. She'd been afraid to sit down for fear she'd damage the upholstery, afraid to drink tea out of the delicate cups one could almost see through, afraid to sleep on sheets finer than any chemise she'd ever worn. The first time Sandy's valet Birchley called her "Miss," she'd looked round wondering whom he was talking to.

But then Sandy's brother had faced exile and Sandy had faced the ruin of his relationship with his brother, and it had been no time to leave him alone. She and Birchley had become allies taking care of Sandy. Mélanie had taken her to her modiste. They'd gone to dine with Mélanie and Malcolm, and though she'd felt hopelessly lost at first, she'd learnt which fork to use with which course and how to take turns talking to the gentleman on either side of her. And after a bit, fine clothes and fine linens hadn't seemed so odd, and her hand had stopped shaking when she poured tea for a guest. But even then, she only went a few select places with Sandy. On nights he dined with his family or went to a ball or a rout or a musicale given by anyone other than the Rannochs or the Davenports or the Carfaxes, she stayed home. Or went to spend the evening playing with the Rannoch children.

"Ben and Nerezza are betrothed," Sandy said.

"That's different." Sometimes with Ben and Nerezza and Kit and Sofia, she felt as though they were part of a set of young couples. But she knew they weren't the same. Nerezza might have a past, but it was far away in Italy. "Sandy, if you think you need to copy Ben—"

"I'm not. I wouldn't make a decision like this to copy anyone. Though I should have offered for you long before Ben offered for Sofia."

"But you didn't. Because you knew it was impossible."

"Bet—" He held out a hand, then let it fall to his side. "I was an idiot. I couldn't see what was in front of me. I was caught up in stupid rules and conventions."

"You weren't. You defied convention by having me move in with you."

"That was nothing. I mean, of course it wasn't nothing. It meant the world to me. Having you here has meant the world to me." He drew a rough breath. "I wouldn't have got through everything with Matt if you hadn't been here."

"And I'm glad I was. I wouldn't have been anywhere else. But it's been almost two years."

"And you're tired of being with me?"

"No, of course not! You can't think that."

"What else am I supposed to think? You want to leave."

"I don't—"

"You don't want to leave?"

"Sandy, we can't go on like this."

"I know. That's why I asked you to marry me. I told you, I should have done it months ago. From the first."

"But you didn't. Because you know it doesn't make sense. You know we aren't meant to be together."

"By whom?"

"By the world. You know what people will say. You know what your parents will say."

"I've been ignoring what my parents have said for months."

"But you knew we couldn't be more than—what we are. You knew better than to try. We were never going to have a fairytale ending."

"I don't want a fairytale ending. I want to live here and now. Bet, please don't punish me for not being clever enough or brave enough to do the right thing sooner."

"God, Sandy, I'm not trying to punish you. I want you to be happy. More than anything."

"And I can't be happy without you." Sandy came up to her again and took her face between his hands. "I knew it from the first. Well, almost from the first. I was three sheets to the wind that first night and didn't know much of anything. Except that I was comfortable with you. Always have been. I can talk to you as I can to no one else. I can laugh with you as I can with no one else. I feel as though I belong with you. Set aside that, what is everything else?"

She gripped his arms instinctively. "Everything else is the world, Sandy. And the world isn't well lost for love, outside of fiction."

"The world wouldn't be lost. We have our friends. We'd make our own world. Bet, please be brave enough not to walk away. You've always been the bravest person I know."

"I'm not brave."

"Sweetheart. You survived in St. Giles. You looked after Nan and Robby. You've faced down my parents. What more bravery can there be?"

"You've read *Pride and Prejudice*. I make Elizabeth Bennet look like the toast of the season."

Sandy frowned. "I'm no Mr. Darcy."

"You're just as well bred."

"I'm not proud. Am I?"

"Of course not. But the way people look at you—"

"That's what I mean. You're brave. You don't care what people think of you. And I'm much braver than I was. I'm braver with you." He glanced away, then looked back at her. "Davenport said— we were talking about Alistair. He seems to want an heir, which I could care less about. But I think—wouldn't you like children some day?"

Tears prickled her eyes. Not having children had been a preoccupation for so long. But she had always liked them. Nan's little girl. The young Rannochs and Davenports and the rest of their friends' children. She'd even thought more than once that if she and Sandy had a child, it wouldn't be impossible. He'd make sure they were cared for. But she also hadn't wanted to burden him. "We can't—"

"The thing is, maybe I'm being too conventional, but it would be better for the children if we were married. Devil take it, it would be better for us to be married. That's what I want, Bet. I want to be with you. Not like this. Well, yes, like this, it's been wonderful. But it would be better if we were married."

"Better?" she said without thinking.

"We could go more places. It would be—official."

"Sandy. We could go fewer places," she said. And then realized for the first time she'd admitted getting married was even a possibility. How strange that she would first admit it as a negative. Though perhaps also not surprising.

"We could go more places together." Sandy reached for her hands. "It would be easier for the children."

"The children are a hypothetical." She tugged her hands away. "And it's not very good for children to see their mother has ruined their father's place in life. Think about *Pride and Prejudice*."

Sandy retained hold of her hands, though normally he would have let her pull away. "That assumes the parents fall out of love, which we wouldn't. But that's not—it's not even about that."

"You don't want children?" she asked, more quickly than she intended.

"No. That is, yes, I do. Very much, I think. But that isn't why I want to marry you. I don't think that's really a good reason to be married. I suppose I haven't been sure of what was a good reason to get married. It always seemed like something one's parents encouraged and one avoided. But—I think maybe the point is"— his fingers tightened over her own—"I want to be with you. I want to know we'll be together forever. I want to say so in front of our friends. Maybe that's what marriage is about."

"Marriage is about fortune and family."

"But is it really? That's what my parents say. But not Malcolm and Mélanie, or Julien and Kitty, or Harry and Cordelia. Or Laura and Raoul."

"They're—"

"Or Ben and Nerezza."

"They're different."

"Why can't we be different? I never could see much sense in getting married for my parents' reasons. Maybe that's why I've avoided even thinking about it. But—" His hands tightened round her own and he drew her closer. "I quite like the idea of getting married for our own reasons. To be together. To say so in front of all our friends. What better reason can there be than that?" He drew a breath. "I mean, I know I'm a bumbling idiot—"

She should pull away. She should point out how those reasons were silly—no, not silly, but powerless against the tide of family and society and all the forces in the world that stood against them. And yet—She released his hands but only to take his face between

148

her hands. "Sandy, you idiot. That is, you aren't an idiot at all. And that's the loveliest thing you've ever said."

"I mean, too often it's about money. Really. That's what it comes down to that my parents want, beneath all the frippery about eligible girls and family alliances. That's what it comes down to for the girls they introduce me to, and their families. That's what it comes down to—"

"That's what it came down to for us at the start."

"No!"

"Sandy. You left me money the next day."

"Well, yes. It would have been bloody rude not to."

"You have a point."

"But that's not what—that's not what it should be about. It should be about us. What we mean to each other. The future we want. Does that sound foolish?"

"Oh, Sandy. It sounds lovely. Like a lovely dream."

"Dreams are important." He turned to the dressing table and picked up the ring he'd given her. He looked down at the aquamarine in the candlelight for a moment, then moved back to her side and held it out to her. "Marry me, Bet. Because I love you. I mean —marry me because—*if* you love me too."

Bet looked into Sandy's familiar eyes. The eyes of the man she loved. The eyes of the man she'd thought she'd have to leave. The eyes of the man she couldn't imagine being without. "Yes."

HISTORICAL NOTES

The protests in Queen Caroline's favor at the time of the royal divorce trial are very real, but the specific events of this story are fictional. In one of her letters, Harriet, Countess Granville, refers to Emily Harriet Wellesley-Pole, Fitzroy Somerset's wife, as Harriet. Based on this, I have always called her Harriet in the series.

THE WHITEHALL CONSPIRACY
EXCERPT

Malcolm and Mélanie Suzanne Rannoch's adventures
in espionage and investigation continue
in Tracy Grant's new historical mystery
The Whitehall Conspiracy
On sale May 2022

PROLOGUE

London

October 1820

*H*ubert Mallinson sat back in his chair and looked at
the man across from him. Strange to be talking like
this. And yet perhaps inevitable. "I assume you have your reasons
for risking this."

"I'm not risking a great deal. No one's looking for me. And you
won't make this public."

"You seem very sure."

"You don't want to force it into the open any more than I do."

He leaned back and took a sip of wine. "It doesn't really make sense that we're enemies you know."

"Doesn't it? I'd have said that that's one of the few things that does make sense."

"We're aligned on most important issues. And we could accomplish a great deal more as allies."

"Assuming I had any desire to help you accomplish anything."

"You've always been a pragmatist. Surely that would depend on what I have to offer."

Hubert reached for his glass but did not take a drink. Much as part of him wanted to leave the room, he had to ask the inevitable question. "What do you have to offer?"

"A profitable alliance that will benefit us both. You have much more in common with me than with Malcolm. And God knows more than with O'Roarke."

"Malcolm's a very good agent. So's O'Roarke if it comes to that."

The other man grimaced. "I suppose I can't deny it. But that doesn't make you allies. You can't deny O'Roarke stands against everything you believe in."

"Oh yes. So does Malcolm. But I don't have to worry about their stabbing me in the back."

"I should think St. Juste would give you enough to think about in that regard."

Carfax took a drink of Bordeaux. A good vintage, he'd give his companion credit for being a good judge of wine. And other things. "You have a point there."

"Not to mention Mélanie Rannoch. She can't possibly be as domestic as she appears."

"I think Mrs. Rannoch would rake you over the coals for suggesting she even appears anything of the sort."

His companion gave a short laugh. "She certainly pulled the wool over Malcolm's eyes. And apparently continues to do so, considering the fact that he's still living with her."

"That might signify that he knows her very well indeed."

"In what way?"

"Malcolm's a number of things, and God knows I've been known to bemoan his impossible delusions about the human race. But I wouldn't discount what's between him and his wife. Or his determination to preserve a marriage that means a great deal to him."

"At what cost?"

"You'll have to ask him that." Hubert pushed his spectacles up.

"I'd assume you think him a fool. But you don't sound that way."

"I wouldn't necessarily play the situation as he's done. But recent events have perhaps given me an appreciation of why a man might see the value in preserving his marriage."

His companion gave a grunt. "Some marriages can't be preserved."

"Very likely. The Rannochs' isn't one of them."

"You sound very sure of that."

Hubert twisted the stem of his glass between his fingers. "I'm sure of few things in life. But oddly, I think I am sure of that."

"She married him to spy on him."

"And managed to deceive all of us. It was ably done. Among other things, Malcolm appreciates that. And Mélanie, I rather think, values having a husband who appreciates her."

"You sound as though you admire her."

"I do," Hubert said, for once speaking the unvarnished truth. "And not in the way most men do. It doesn't mean I trust her. But I'd rather have her at my back than you."

A shadow flickered across his companion's face. He took a drink of wine. "I thought you said you were interested in what I had to offer. Or was that all a hum?"

"Oh, I'm interested. It wouldn't be prudent not to explore all options."

His companion leaned forwards, "I can help you secure the

king's case. There's a lot to be said for a grateful monarch. It will ensure the Whigs and Radicals retreat and give them no chance of turning the royal divorce to their advantage."

"I'm listening,"

"You can send that upstart Brougham packing with his tail between his legs."

"Brougham has a tendency to bounce back like a rubber ball. But go on."

"It will let you consolidate your power against Castlereagh and Sidmouth and anyone else who's been encroaching."

Hubert stretched his legs out under the table and cupped his hands round his glass. "I wasn't aware that anyone had been encroaching. I must be slipping."

"You know damn well you're not slipping. But you can't deny certain people have been taking advantage of the recent changes in our circumstances."

Hubert's hands tightened round the wine glass, though he flattered himself no one could tell. "My power never rested on being Lord Carfax."

"But you turned being Carfax to your advantage. You're good at turning things to your advantage. I'm offering you the chance to do so again."

Hubert took a deliberate drink of wine. "And in exchange?"

His companion reached for the bottle and refilled their glasses. "I want what Fanny got for O'Roarke and Mélanie. I want a pardon."

"For what?"

"For everything."

"I don't even know what everything is."

"No, that's true. You don't."

"It's asking a great deal."

"If the king gets what he wants it will be worth a great deal."

"To him."

"And to you if you bring it about."

155

Hubert twisted the stem of his glass between his fingers. "You could of course be setting all this up to ruin me. You've tried to enough in the past."

"That's because you were trying to destroy us. If you join us you wouldn't be an enemy anymore. After all isn't joining us what you always wanted?"

"Joining you? I wanted to stop you from wreaking havoc on Britain and the Continent. Just like O'Roarke and Malcolm and their Leveller friends."

"Are you sure it wasn't jealousy of your brother?"

The word lingered in the air. "I never paid enough heed to my brother to be jealous."

His companion leaned back in his chair. "Can you really say you wouldn't have joined us all those years ago if we'd asked you?"

"Oh, I daresay I would have done. To keep an eye on you. I daresay O'Roarke would have done for the same reasons."

"You're talking about O'Roarke as though he's a friend."

"He is after a fashion. I'm not particularly pleased that you've tried to have him killed."

"You've done the same yourself."

"Possibly. With better cause. I wouldn't do so now unless things changed drastically."

"Things have a way of changing, don't they?" His companion took a drink of wine. "And given our current circumstances, I'd have no reason to move against you. Not if I could secure your cooperation."

Hubert held his companion's gaze. "Unless you wanted to destroy me for the same reason you wanted to destroy O'Roarke."

His companion returned his gaze. His hand remained steady on the wine glass, but Hubert fancied it cost him an effort to keep it so. "In your case it was a mission. In Arabella's too."

"Difficult to tell sometimes where the mission leaves off. I imagine Mélanie could tell us something about that. And I imagine Malcolm and my wife could tell us something about whether or not it's being a mission negates the impact on others involved."

"Don't make the mistake of confusing me with Malcolm, who for all his apparent coldness is entirely too likely to dwell on the emotions involved. O'Roarke has always been my opponent. Our tactics could never align. Yours and mine could. That's all it comes down to."

"There's rarely any 'all' anything comes down to. And while I agree it's a tiresome waste to dwell too much on emotions, I think one ignores them at one's peril. I'd never make the mistake of assuming you were entirely rational."

"I think I should be insulted by that."

"Don't be. I don't claim I could be entirely rational if you'd seduced Amelia." Hubert's fingers froze on the frame of his spectacles.

"No," his companion said. "That never occurred to me. Proof perhaps of my own rationality in such matters."

"Or of the fact that you can deceive even yourself." Hubert took a drink of wine, gaze steady on the other man's face. "Take it from one who knows."

"You're talking like a fool, Hubert."

"We're all fools at times." Hubert continued to watch the other man. "For what it's worth. I can imagine Arabella upsetting a man's best laid plans. She'd be worth it."

The other man's fingers tightened round his wine glass.

"That isn't what she meant to me," Hubert said. "Or I to her. But I liked her. And there aren't many people I'd say that about."

His companion tossed down a drink of wine and drummed his fingers on the table. "You're very good at prevaricating. Which I admit can be a useful talent. But this is a business proposition. I wouldn't attack you or O'Roarke or anyone else simply for personal reasons. Do you want what I have to offer? If not, I'll make other arrangements."

Hubert sat back in his chair and took a slow, deliberate drink of wine. Because what he said could change everything.

CHAPTER ONE

Scandalous. Shocking. Impressive. Remember the evidence about the bedsheets? Non mi ricordo!

The fragments carried through the crowd on the stairs outside the House of Lords chamber, thick as a flurry of autumn leaves.

"What's more exciting?" Cordelia Davenport asked over the patter of voices and footfalls on marble stairs. "Having your words spoken on stage at the Tavistock or in the House of Lords?"

Mélanie Rannoch tightened her grip on her son Colin's hand as they negotiated the crowd on the stairs outside the House of Lords. "Those were hardly my words just now."

"Some of them were," Laura Dudley said. "I can attest that you and Malcolm spent hours editing Brougham's speech."

"We maybe sharpened it a bit." Mélanie righted her bonnet as someone jostled into her. Parliament was as crowded today as the Tavistock or Covent Garden on an opening night. Perhaps not surprising given the drama playing out, though it would be difficult to say it was tragedy or farce. Henry Brougham had just given the opening speech for the defense in the trial before the Lords in which George IV, the new, as yet uncrowned king, was attempting to divorce his long-estranged wife, Caroline.

"Where's Aunt Kitty?" Colin asked.

"We're here." Kitty Mallinson and her elder son Leo slipped between two men earnestly debating the merits of Brougham's speech. The four women had each brought their eldest children to the ladies' gallery to hear the opening. Mad as the events unfolding in London now were, they were shaping history, and it seemed important for the children to see it unfold.

More people were spilling onto the stairs. Mélanie caught Laura's daughter Emily's hand in her free hand while Cordelia and Kitty joined hands, and the four of them and the children tried to stay close together. It was harder than trying to keep a group of fighters together in a skirmish.

They turned a corner and were halfway down the last flight of stairs when the crowd stopped abruptly. A dark-coated man in front of her surged backwards, hurtling into her. Her half boots skidded on the step.

"That man fell!" Colin yelled.

Mélanie could see a man's bootlegs a few steps down. Someone screamed. Mélanie cast a quick glance at Laura. Laura grabbed Colin's hand. Mélanie pushed forwards and dropped down beside the man who had fallen. He was sprawled over the steps at a haphazard angle. His blue eyes were open but already glazed. She put her hand to his chest to feel for his pulse and felt something damp and sticky. Blood was seeping through the side of his waistcoat. She tugged off her spencer and pressed it to the man's chest. "Can you hear me? Try to stay with me."

He shuddered. Someone else screamed. She pressed her hands to his chest, heard him gasp, saw the light go from his eyes. She looked up to see a circle of people gathered round and met Kitty's gaze. "He's dead."

"For someone used to weapons, I'm coming to appreciate the power of the spoken word," Julien Mallinson murmured, leaning close to Malcolm Rannoch to make his voice heard in the crush outside the Lords chamber. "I don't know how it seemed from the gallery, but you could have heard a pin drop on the floor."

"In the gallery as well. But it won't be enough. Not on its own." Malcolm scanned the crowd. Probably fruitless to try to catch sight of Mélanie, Laura, Cordy, and Kitty and the children in the thong. He'd told Mel he'd see her at home, since he'd be caught up in the endless Whig discussions at Brooks's after today's session.

"They're all good at navigating chaos," Harry Davenport said, reading his thoughts. "Better than we are. This is nothing to the crush at a successful ball."

That was true. And no need to worry, Malcolm told himself. London was on edge, but it seemed excessive to fear violence inside the Houses of Parliament. So far the protests had been confined to the streets. And it was the Tory opposition and people like his former spymaster, Julien's uncle Hubert Mallinson, who worried about the protests, while he was inclined to think it was a release of very understandable frustrations. But recent events had left him on edge.

"A lot of long Tory faces." Raoul O'Roarke, Malcolm's father, slid through the crowd to join them. "At the risk of sounding small-minded, I confess it's quite satisfying."

"Nothing wrong with that," Malcolm said. "But however dour they look, we haven't won anything unless they change their votes."

Harry clapped him on the shoulder. "Take your victories while you can. Your side has at least won the day. And you and Mélanie helped hone the winning speech."

"Just round the edges," Malcolm said.

The crowd had eddied enough to allow them to inch forwards. Julien was slightly in the lead. He went still suddenly, nearly making Malcolm stumble. "Did you hear that?"

"What?" Malcolm asked. Julien had catlike senses.

"A scream."

"Probably Tory frustration," Harry said. "Though it's difficult to tell the Tory screams of frustration from Whig shouts of glee."

"No." Julien was frowning with a seriousness he rarely showed. "I don't know if it was a Whig or a Tory, but someone shouted 'murder.'"

~

"Jeremy. Thank God." Mélanie moved to the door as Jeremy Roth came into the sitting room the House of Lords ushers had shown them into.

"I was in the gallery." Roth crossed to her side and gripped hands. An unusual lack of restraint for him, especially on duty. Roth, a Bow Street Runner, was usually very conscious of his role, for all he had become a personal friend. "We were worried about trouble though this wasn't what we had in mind. I'm sorry you stumbled across this, though also relieved." He glanced at the end of the room where Laura and Cordy were sitting with the children, then looked back at Mélanie. "Do you know who he is?"

"We'd never seen him before he tumbled down dead in front of us," Mélanie said. "He'd been stabbed in the side. Probably with a thin blade."

"It's the sort of thing my husband used to be known to do," Kitty said in a cool voice. "But Julien was still in the chamber. And he wouldn't. Not now. Not without cause anyway. And I don't think he had it."

Roth nodded.

"You don't know who he is?" Mélanie asked.

Roth shook his head. "No one's come forwards to identify him. His coat is well-tailored but his pockets were bare of identifying information."

"I know," Mélanie said. "I searched them before the ushers hurried us away. He looked to be in late twenties. Maybe early thirties." She had an image of an image of high cheekbones, a smattering of freckles, tousled auburn hair. Details she'd scarcely taken in in her focus on trying to save the victim but had registered at the back of her mind.

"I can get you another look at the body," Roth said. "We need to identify him before we go any further. We thought about closing the doors, but it would only have led to panic, and by then the killer was almost certainly long gone."

"Quite certainly," a familiar voice said from the door.

Julien was standing there. Malcolm pushed past him and came forwards to grip Mélanie by the shoulders.

"We're all right, darling," Mélanie said, closing her fingers on his elbows.

"We were in the wrong place at the wrong time," Cordelia said, looking round to meet Harry's gaze, as he and Raoul followed Julien and Malcolm into the room.

"Or possibly the right place at the right time," Kitty said. "I imagine few other people today would have been as prepared to deal with a murder."

"You'll have to Investigate," Colin said.

"Malcolm and Julien can't," Emily said. "They have to save the queen."

"He didn't say anything?" Roth asked Mélanie.

She shook her head. "He was barely conscious by the time I got to him. And we didn't see anything before he fell. If only—"

She broke off as the door burst open again to admit Hopkins, one of the Bow Street patrols who worked with Roth.

"Have you learned the victim's identity?" Roth asked.

"No." Hopkins pushed his fair hair back from his face. He had always struck Mélanie as quite matter-of-fact, but now his blue eyes were wide with shock. "But there's been an unexpected development. To own the truth, sir, I'm not sure what to make of it. But I think you'll have to send for the prime minister."

ALSO BY TRACY GRANT

Traditional Regencies

WIDOW'S GAMBIT

FRIVOLOUS PRETENCE

THE COURTING OF PHILIPPA

Lescaut Quartet

DARK ANGEL

SHORES OF DESIRE

SHADOWS OF THE HEART

RIGHTFULLY HIS

The Rannoch Fraser Mysteries

HIS SPANISH BRIDE

LONDON INTERLUDE

VIENNA WALTZ

IMPERIAL SCANDAL

THE PARIS AFFAIR

THE PARIS PLOT

BENEATH A SILENT MOON

THE BERKELEY SQUARE AFFAIR

THE MAYFAIR AFFAIR

INCIDENT IN BERKELEY SQUARE

LONDON GAMBIT

MISSION FOR A QUEEN

GILDED DECEIT

ABOUT THE AUTHOR

Tracy Grant studied British history at Stanford University and received the Firestone Award for Excellence in Research for her honors thesis on shifting conceptions of honor in late-fifteenth-century England. She lives in the San Francisco Bay Area with her young daughter and three cats. In addition to writing, Tracy works for the Merola Opera Program, a professional training program for opera singers, pianists, and stage directors. Her real life heroine is her daughter Mélanie, who is very cooperative about Mummy's writing time. She is currently at work on her next book chronicling the adventures of Malcolm and Mélanie Suzanne Rannoch. Visit her on the Web at www.tracygrant.org

Cover photo by Kristen Loken.

Made in the USA
Coppell, TX
29 March 2022

75726648R00105